Note to Readers

While the Fisk and Allerton families are fictional, the events that surround this story actually happened. Baseball was a fairly new game. *Pitchers* were called *hurlers,* and *batters* were called *strikers.* The curve ball hadn't been invented, and there was disagreement about whether stealing a base was legal.

Decades of arguing about slavery were about to end with the outbreak of the Civil War. Because Cincinnati sat across the Ohio River from the Southern states and had many ties with both the North and the South, this conflict was personal. Everyone who lived in Cincinnati knew people on both sides of the battle.

TIME
for
BATTLE

Susan Martins Miller

PUBLISHING, INC.

Uhrichsville, Ohio

© MCMXCVII by Barbour Publishing, Inc.

ISBN 1-57748-260-3

Published by Barbour Publishing, Inc.
       P.O. Box 719
       Uhrichsville, Ohio 44683
       http://www.barbourbooks.com

ecpa Member of the
Evangelical Christian
Publishers Association

Printed in the United States of America.

Cover illustration by Peter Pagano.
Inside illustrations by Adam Wallenta.

CHAPTER 1

The New Boy

"Ow!"

Daria Fisk leaped to her feet, whirled around, and scowled into the open field behind her. She had been sitting in the shade of the oak tree, minding her own business, when something bonked her on the head. With two fingers, she tested the tender spot. A lump swelled under Daria's reddish brown hair. At her feet lay the weapon that had attacked her—a baseball.

"This is great," she said aloud. "Not only am I as hot as I have ever been, but now I'm going to have the biggest headache I have ever had."

She slumped against the tree and sprawled her legs out in front of her. The white pinafore covering her everyday dress was smudged with dirt in three places. Daria hated the ruffles on the pinafore, but her mother would not make her another one until she outgrew this one. By then, she would be twelve and too old for pinafores.

Sighing, she reached for the clay jar she had carried with her all afternoon. August in Cincinnati was always hot, and 1860 was no different. Daria never went anywhere without a jar of water. She tilted her head back to welcome the refreshment. But the jar was empty. Daria tossed it into the grass with a thud. Frustrated, she stood up again, scooped up the baseball, and heaved it as far as she could.

"Keep your stupid ball!" she screamed at the air.

"It's not a stupid ball, and you just lost it."

At the sound of the strange voice with the strong accent, Daria looked up and saw a boy. He stood about thirty feet away from her. He was not moving. He just stood and stared at her. She tilted her head to one side and inspected him. He was about Daria's age—ten—but she did not recognize him. And she was certain that she knew everyone in her neighborhood.

They stood and stared at each other for several minutes. Slowly, they began moving toward each other.

Finally the boy spoke. "That was my ball you threw. Now you've lost it in the high grass."

"I did not lose your ball," Daria retorted, her hands crossed in front of her. "If you had controlled it a little better in the first place, it would not have gotten lost."

"I did control it. I hit it exactly where I wanted to hit it." He seemed quite proud of himself.

"On my head?" Daria began marching toward the boy. "You wanted to hit me in the head with your baseball?"

"No, I'm sorry, I didn't mean to do that. I just meant that I was aiming at the oak tree. So I was in control of the ball, you see."

Daria noticed for the first time that the boy had a baseball bat cocked over one shoulder.

"Did you carve your own bat?" Daria asked.

"Sure did. This used to be an ax handle."

Daria nodded. Her brother David had made a bat out of a shovel handle.

"Where were you hitting from?" she asked skeptically.

The boy turned and pointed. "From over there. The tree is left field."

Daria scanned the field. "You hit it a long way."

The boy grinned. "Yep. Sorry you happened to be under the tree just then."

"It's too hot to play baseball," Daria muttered.

"It's never too hot to play baseball. Or too cold."

"You sound like my brother. All he ever thinks about is baseball."

"Now you've gone and lost my ball," the boy said. "I knew it would be under the tree because that's where I was aiming. But you had to go and throw it into the field."

Daria reached up to feel the lump on her head. "I'll do the same thing if you ever hit me on the head with it again."

"Well, are you going to help me look for it?"

"Can't think why I should. I don't even know you."

Daria crossed her arms across her chest and looked at him evenly.

"I have forgotten my manners," the boy said with a drawl. "My name is DJ Baxter."

"Why haven't I ever met you before? I know everyone around here."

"We've just moved from South Carolina." There was that drawl again. "My family has been in South Carolina for a hundred years. We have a huge cotton plantation there, one of the biggest in South Carolina."

South Carolina! Daria had known a few families from across the Ohio River in Kentucky or West Virginia. But she had never met anyone from as far south as South Carolina. No wonder he talked in such a funny way.

"So what are you doing here?" she asked.

"My father just bought a shoe factory in Cincinnati," he answered. "We were going to move to New Hampshire, but after the shoemakers' strike there last spring, Daddy decided Cincinnati was a safer investment."

"Do you have slaves on your plantation?" Daria did not mean to blurt out her question, but she was so curious she could not hold it in.

"Of course," DJ answered. "Who do you suppose plants and picks all that cotton? My parents?"

Daria inspected the boy again. His blond hair hung long under his blue cap. His gray eyes met her gaze evenly and confidently. He swung the bat down from his shoulders and tapped the ground with it.

"You could tell me your name now," he said.

"Daria Fisk, although it's not any of your business."

"Now that we've been properly introduced," he said,

8

"I've got to find that ball, and I think you should help me look."

Reluctantly Daria gestured off to the right. "I think it went that way."

Using his bat as a walking stick, DJ thrashed through the grass. "Well? Come on."

Daria shuffled behind him, half-heartedly looking for the ball.

"My brother is good with a bat, too," Daria said.

Daria could picture David tramping through a field just like DJ was doing, hitting a ball, retrieving it, hitting it again. He never got tired of baseball. Daria did. She liked baseball, but she thought about other things, too. David only thought about baseball.

"Maybe I should meet your brother," DJ said. "We could see just how good he is."

"He's good, all right," Daria insisted. Even though she got frustrated with David sometimes, he was her twin brother. She was not going to let this stranger from South Carolina think David could not hit a baseball. She asked, "Do you know where the school is?"

"A square brick building with red doors?"

Daria nodded. "That's it. Meet me there tomorrow afternoon, right after lunch. I'll bring David. There's a better field to play in."

DJ nodded. "Sure. I'll be there. I need to meet some boys to play ball with. If I can find my ball, that is."

Daria's toe hit what she thought was a rock. But it moved.

"Look what I found," she said, as she bent over to pick it up.

9

DJ quickly took it from her. "Don't get any ideas about heaving it away again."

Daria looked into DJ's gray eyes and laughed. "We'll see you tomorrow," she said as she turned toward home.

Walking home, Daria shook her head. She could hardly believe she had met someone from South Carolina. What would her family think? Uncle Tim thought that a person had to be crazy to believe slavery was right. He was always looking for ways to help slaves. He argued for laws that would make sure that slavery would not spread to new states as they joined the Union.

Daria's parents agreed with him, of course. They just did not talk about it in public as much as Uncle Tim did. But Kevin Fisk, her father, had joined the Republican Party. He planned to cast his vote for Abraham Lincoln as the next president of the United States. The election was only a few weeks away. Daria's parents and uncles talked about it all the time.

What was the South really like? Daria wondered. Cincinnati had some black people—more than most northern cities. Most of the time, they kept to their own part of town, between the canal and the river. Sometimes Daria would see black people when she was out shopping with her mother. No one seemed to mind that they had settled in Cincinnati, although Uncle Tim told stories of earlier times when the white people of Cincinnati had tried to drive the blacks out.

But it was still nothing like the South. DJ Baxter was from South Carolina. He was used to the idea of slavery. He acted like he had a right to make all those other people pick cotton so his family could be rich. But DJ did not look rich—at least not what Daria thought rich people would look like. No fancy carriage waited to take him home. His baseball was just as ragged as her brother's. And he needed a haircut.

With her empty clay jar tucked under her arm, Daria scooted along the streets that took her home. When she reached the Fisk house, she was not at all surprised to see her mother and her sister sitting in the rocking chairs on the front porch. In the afternoons, this was the coolest place to be.

"Hi, Mama. Hi, Tina."

"I was wondering when you would wander home," Mama said to her youngest daughter. "I see your pinafore needs washing again."

"It's a dumb old pinafore, and I hate it!" Daria slumped into a chair between her mother and her sister.

"Daria!" Mama said sternly. "I don't like to hear you speak that way."

Daria stuck her chin out but said nothing.

"Where have you been off to this afternoon?" Tina asked.

"Just around."

"Oh."

Tina was nineteen. She did not ask a lot of nosy questions. So no one asked her any nosy questions. Daria thought this was a good arrangement.

"Did you have your sewing circle today?" Daria asked. Since Tina went to a sewing circle meeting every week, Daria did not think that was a nosy question. She did sometimes wonder what Tina did with all the things she sewed. She never seemed to make anything for herself.

But Daria never asked. That would be nosy.

"Yes. I learned a new stitch," Tina said. "I'll have to teach it to you."

Daria made a face. She had to learn to sew. All girls did. But she did not have to like it.

"Is Daddy home?" Daria asked.

"No," her mother answered. "He had several appointments at the clinic this afternoon. He said not to expect him until late."

"People always get sick at suppertime," Daria commented.

"Your father is a doctor," Mama said, "and he cannot control when people are going to need to be taken care of."

"Can't Meg take care of the people who come late?"

"Your cousin is a nurse, Daria. She's a great help to your father, but he's still the doctor. You'll just have to be more understanding of his schedule."

Daria suddenly remembered DJ.

"Where's David?" she asked.

"I left him in the kitchen," Tina said. "He was looking for something to eat. He said he couldn't wait until supper."

Mama chuckled. "He's just like your brother Charles in that way," she said. "They both eat as much as the rest of us put together."

"Is Charles coming home for supper?" Daria asked.

"His shift at the railroad station should be over soon," her mother answered. "He'll be along."

Charles was seventeen. He was as crazy about the railroad as David was about baseball. For years he had spent all his spare time at the railroad station or walking the rails, learning everything he could about routes and train cars. Finally he was old enough to get a job at the railroad.

"I have to talk to David." Daria got up, pulled open the front door, and went in the house.

In the kitchen, David was just finishing a piece of cherry pie.

"Does Mama know you ate that?" Daria asked.

David shrugged and kept on chewing.

"Did you leave anything for the rest of us?" Daria asked.

David made a face. Daria sat down at the table across from him.

"I met someone today that you have to meet."

"Who says?"

"Come on, David. You'll like this kid. He's crazy about baseball, just like you. And I think he's a pretty good striker. He hit the ball clear across the field."

David lifted his eyes briefly. "What's his name?"

"DJ."

David stopped chewing and looked at Daria for the first time since she entered the room. "You mean TJ."

"No, DJ. DJ Baxter."

"Is he about our age, blond hair, wears a blue cap?"

"Yes, that's him."

"I've met him already. And his name is TJ."

"I'm sure it's DJ. And he didn't say he knew you."

"You need to let Papa clean the wax out of your ears so you can hear properly. His name is TJ, and I do so know him. Met him at the schoolyard two days ago."

"DJ!"

"TJ!"

"DJ!"

"TJ!"

As their voices grew louder, they rose to their feet.

The kitchen door swung open.

"What in the world is going on in here?" Mama demanded.

Daria and David glared at each other, ignoring their mother.

"Come to the schoolyard with me after lunch tomorrow," Daria said. "I'll show you."

"I'll come," David retorted, "but I'll show you!"

"I'll show you!"

"Twins, twins!" Mama sighed in exasperation.

CHAPTER 2

The Baxter Twins

"I'm not deaf, you know," David declared as he got up from the lunch table the next day. "I learned to talk at the same time you did."

He charged ahead of his sister out the door toward their school. His thatch of brown hair flopped to the side of his head.

Daria sped up. "Maybe you need to let Papa clean the wax out of your ears so you can hear. His name is DJ."

"What kind of name is DJ, anyway? That's just letters."

"It's the same kind of name as TJ—except DJ is the right name."

"Aw, never mind!"

Daria smiled to herself. She knew she could outlast

David in an argument. When they were little, they used to argue about the flavor of their candy or who could eat more of their mother's fresh-baked bread. And Daria always outlasted David, squeezing in the last word before their mother silenced them.

They came to the end of their block and turned the corner toward the school. With a scowl fixed on his face, David kept his eyes straight ahead. Daria kept pace with David, but she stayed a few steps behind him. It would not matter who got to the schoolyard first. Daria knew she was right.

For nine more blocks they continued on. Finally the square brick building where they went to school was in sight. Even from a distance, Daria could see the slim figure of a boy leaning against the wall.

"There he is," Daria said loudly. "There's DJ."

"You mean there's TJ."

They approached the boy. He was tossing a baseball in the air and catching it with one hand. A bat was propped against the wall of the school.

"DJ!" Daria called loudly. She raised her arm and waved it widely.

The boy returned the wave. "I wasn't sure if you had come earlier," he called out.

Daria looked at David triumphantly. This was DJ all right. She quickened her steps to reach him first.

DJ pointed at David. "Is this the big shot striker you told me about?"

David raised his shoulders and dropped them madly. "Don't act like you don't know me. I talked to you three days ago. You're the boy from South Carolina."

"I'm from South Carolina, but I've never laid eyes on you before."

"But we had a long conversation about baseball and school and lots of other stuff."

DJ shook his head. "I just met your sister yesterday. She tells me you're pretty good with a bat. I wanted to see for myself."

"Is this some kind of crazy trick?" David's brown eyes bulged. "Why are you acting like you don't know me?"

"Because I don't."

"Yes, you do."

"No, I don't."

"But I do," said an identical voice. From around the corner of the school, another boy appeared. "Hello, David."

"TJ!"

"Yep, that's me." The boy grinned.

David turned back to the first boy. "Then you really are DJ."

Daria poked her brother with her elbow. "See? I told you I was right."

Daria was just as surprised as David, but she'd never admit it to him. Before them stood identical boys, both with longish blond hair, both with gray eyes, both with high cheekbones and slightly pointed chins. They even dressed in the same dark green trousers and brown shirts. Twins. Identical twins.

Daria collapsed in the grass laughing. "There are two of you! You're twins."

TJ and DJ looked at each other and grinned.

"Turner James Baxter."

"Donald James Baxter."

Then DJ looked back at Daria, rolling around in the grass. "But why are you laughing so hard?" he asked.

Daria pointed at David. "Us, too. We're twins. Not identical, of course, but twins."

The Baxter twins examined the Fisk twins. The Fisk twins examined the Baxter twins. Four brown eyes looked into four gray eyes.

"This certainly explains things," David announced. "Do you do this to people all the time?"

TJ grinned. "As often as we can."

David looked from one identical twin to the other. "You two look exactly alike. And you sound just the same. How will we ever tell you apart?"

"Just wait till y'all get to know us," DJ said. "Y'all find out that I'm the nice one."

"But I'm the smart one," TJ retorted. He swatted his brother on the shoulder. "And I taught DJ everything he knows about baseball."

David shook his head, confused. Daria was deciding for herself. She could tell them apart already. DJ's eyes were a softer gray, with a steady expression. TJ's flickered with a bright excitement.

"Who's older?" David asked.

"Me, by nine and a half minutes," DJ said, pointing proudly to his chest.

Daria grimaced. "David never lets me forget that he beat me being born by seven minutes."

"Don't you hate sharing a birthday?" David asked.

"Yes," said DJ, "and everyone calls us 'the twins' instead of by our given names."

"That happens to us, too," Daria said. "What will people

do when all four of us are together?"

"We didn't know any other twins in South Carolina," DJ said.

"Did you play baseball in South Carolina?" David asked.

"Of course, at least with each other," DJ answered. "I think baseball is more popular here in the North, but we've always liked it."

"We make Mariah play with us," TJ said, laughing. "She doesn't like it, but she has to do it."

"Why?" Daria asked. She certainly did not do everything her brothers asked her to do.

"She has to," TJ said again.

"But why?" Daria repeated. "Why do you make your sister play if she doesn't want to?"

TJ scoffed. "Mariah's not our sister! Mariah is just a slave. If we tell Mama we want Mariah to play with us, then she has to do it. Actually, she's pretty good. She's got a good throwing arm."

DJ chuckled. "That's because she's had so much experience playing the outfield and throwing the ball back in after we hit it."

"That's why I tell Mama to make her play. I hate playing in the outfield."

"We should bring her out here," DJ said. "She hasn't played with us since we got to Cincinnati."

Daria almost always had something to say. But just then, she was speechless. The Baxter twins had come from South Carolina, a state where slavery was legal, and they were proud that their family owned hundreds of slaves. Now Daria discovered that they had brought one of the slaves with them to Cincinnati. She could not imagine what it would be like to be a slave in Cincinnati. The only black people she had ever met were free blacks.

"Are we going to stand around and gab, or are we going to play ball?" TJ tossed a ball high in the air. DJ snatched it out of the air on the way back down.

"Let's play!" David said. "Who wants to hurl?"

"TJ's got a good arm," DJ said. "You can strike first, David. I'll catch behind."

"What about me?" Daria asked.

The boys looked at one another and shrugged.

"You can play the outfield, I guess," David finally said.

Daria resisted the urge to argue. She would show David how important it was to have a good player in the outfield.

David pointed out the landmarks that he usually used for bases. First base was a tree stump. Second base was a flat rock. Third base was a bare spot in the grass. And a broken fence board marked home plate. TJ positioned himself midway between home plate and second base. David picked up a bat and practiced swinging. DJ squatted behind home plate. When Daria looked at him, he pointed at the outfield—her assigned position. She was starting to understand what Mariah must feel like. But she went to midfield without a word.

TJ leaned over and touched his toes a few times, then stretched his arms. He was ready to pitch.

David spread his feet apart, raised the bat above his shoulder, and stared at TJ.

TJ cranked his arm backward faster than anyone Daria had ever seen. After three times around, he stepped forward and let go of the ball.

The first pitch whizzed past David and smacked into DJ's waiting hands. David hardly saw it. He had never seen such a fast pitch. His brown eyes widened as he looked at TJ again. He dug his feet into the earth more solidly and waited for the next pitch.

From the outfield, Daria squinted into the sun. David looked nervous.

The next pitch came. This was just as fast as the first pitch, but David was ready to swing. Grunting as he moved, he swung as hard and evenly as he could. Too late. Instead of the crack of the bat, all he heard was the swish of the air. He had missed.

He looked over his shoulder and saw the ball in DJ's hands. DJ grinned. "I told you he had a good arm." He lobbed the ball back to his brother.

David got ready again. He was all business now, determined to hit the next pitch. This time, he anticipated TJ's pitch. As TJ got ready to release the ball, David started his swing. By the time the ball got to the plate, David's bat was right over the plate, ready to meet the ball.

Crack! It worked! The ball sailed up over TJ's head, out into left field. David started running toward the tree stump.

From center field, Daria scrambled to get to the ball. Running in the tall grass was difficult in her skirt and pinafore. She had no hope of getting to left field before the ball got there. And she didn't. Instead of catching it, which she knew she should have, she chased it. By the time she had picked it up, David was rounding the rock at second base and was on his way to third. As hard as she could, Daria heaved the ball back into the infield.

But no one was really interested in the ball. This was not a game. It was just practice. Neither DJ nor TJ made an effort to get the ball and tag David. Instead, they cheered his hit.

DJ and David traded places. The lump on Daria's head reminded her that DJ could hit a ball just as far and hard as David. She backed up a few steps.

DJ was more used to TJ's pitching. He hit the first ball his brother threw. It was a line drive, headed straight for the pitcher. TJ ducked just in time, and the ball whizzed past him into midfield.

But Daria was in left field now. Once again she scrambled to keep the ball from rolling past her and heaved it back into the infield.

David took another turn at bat, then DJ, then David, then DJ. TJ seemed to love pitching. Daria was getting tired of running around the outfield.

Daria threw the ball back to the infield after DJ's last hit and then paused to rub her shoulder. It was then that she noticed a fifth person on the field. A young, thin black woman stood on the first base line and gestured toward the Baxter boys. She was saying something to them. TJ kicked the dirt. DJ turned and motioned that Daria should come in.

She trotted toward the pitcher's mound as fast as the heat and her weariness would let her.

"Mama sent Mariah to fetch us," DJ said. "We have to go home."

"But we can do this every day," TJ said.

"Yeah," David said enthusiastically. "Maybe we can even figure out a way to play real games."

"You'll need even teams for games," Daria said, as she caught her breath.

"I know, but there are only three of us. We'll have to find someone else."

Daria crossed her arms in disgust. "I count four of us right now!"

"You?" David asked. "You want to play baseball?"

"Why not?"

"You're a girl."

"Yes, and I've been running all over the outfield for you."

"I don't know," David muttered.

"It's all right," DJ said, jumping in. "She can be my partner."

Daria caught DJ's eyes. She was suspicious. But he seemed to mean what he said.

"All right," Daria agreed.

"Good," said TJ. "It's settled. We can come back tomorrow and play a game. We'll make sure Mama will let us stay longer."

"I'll meet you right here tomorrow morning," David said.

"You're forgetting about the picnic," Daria said.

David groaned. "That's right. The church picnic is tomorrow. We always go."

"Anyone is welcome at the picnic," Daria said.

David's eyes brightened. "That's right. You could come. Your whole family could come. At the picnic, we could even find enough players for whole teams."

Mariah had been standing by patiently. Now she spoke. "Your mama gonna be lookin' for ya," she said softly. "We best be goin'.'" She turned to go and gave the Baxter boys a stern look.

"The picnic starts at ten in the morning in the field behind the church," David said quickly. "It's two blocks west of here. Do you know where that is?"

"No problem," DJ said. "We'll be there."

With a wave the twin boys headed off toward home.

CHAPTER 3

Problems at the Picnic

The horse neighed gratefully as Daria offered an apple. She stroked the mare's neck and laced her fingers in its thick mane. It was a nice day for a picnic, she decided— not as hot as it had been all week, with a bit of a breeze.

Daria stood in the row of black carriages at one end of the meadow behind the church. When her family unloaded the carriage and went to find their place in the meadow, Daria had lingered behind. From the carriage line, Daria could see everything. And she could be looking for the Baxters.

The church members gathered for their annual picnic.

Girls in pinafores and sun bonnets ran through the grass with their brothers in cotton trousers and suspenders. A black and white dog trotted after a barefooted little boy, who reminded Daria of a smaller version of David. A straw hat bobbed on the child's head. If anyone was ready for a picnic, it was that little boy.

Quilts covered the meadow, forming one giant quilt in Daria's mind. It reminded her of the little bits of cloth her mother pieced together into quilts for the Fisk family. Daria still used the green one her mother had made when Daria and David were four.

Sewing, especially quilting, seemed like such hard work to Daria. Her stitches were never straight enough, and her thread was always in a knot. No matter how hard Tina tried to teach her, Daria's projects ended up in a wad stuffed into a sewing basket. She had not inherited her mother's talent, like Tina had. Pamela Fisk loved to quilt. She made quilt after quilt, cheerfully giving many of them away as soon as they were finished.

Nearly every quilt in the grass had a basket of food waiting. Cold chicken, roast beef, bread, garden vegetables, summer fruits, and clay jars of cool drinks peeked out from under the cloths that covered the baskets. Daria hoped her mother had brought lemonade or tea to drink and not just water.

Daria's stomach grumbled. She looked up at the sun and winced. It was a long time until lunch would be served.

A carriage rumbled behind her. Daria turned around to look at it. Two blond heads leaned out the side.

"Hi, Daria!"

"Hello, TJ. Hello, DJ."

The carriage slowed and then stopped. Daria ran over and stood next to it.

"Mama, this is Daria Fisk," one of the boys said as he tumbled out of the carriage. He looked around. "Where's David?"

"He's off trying to find enough people for a game," Daria said. She had decided it was DJ who had spoken first.

"Great!" The other boy jumped down. "We're ready to play."

When she saw the intensity of the second boy's eyes—which had to be TJ—Daria was sure she had the Baxter twins straight. Now all she had to do was keep them straight all day.

"Boys, y'all will mind your manners."

Daria was surprised that a Southern drawl could sound stern. She watched as Deborah Baxter appeared in the opening of the carriage. Dutifully her two sons offered their hands to assist her down. Her dress of deep purple cloth, with a hooped skirt and lavender trim around the bottom, billowed out ahead of her. On her head was a large straw hat covered with bows, feathers, and flowers. It tied under her chin with purple ribbon that matched her dress. Daria had never seen a hat quite so large. The brim shielded Mrs. Baxter's face so well that Daria could hardly tell what she looked like.

"I'm pleased to meet you, Daria," Mrs. Baxter said. "This is my husband, Mr. Baxter." She gestured vaguely toward Ned Baxter, who was busy hitching the horse. He nodded politely at Daria.

"The twins have told us all about you and your brother," Mrs. Fisk continued. "I understand you are twins as well."

Daria nodded.

"It was most gracious of you to invite us to the picnic. Mr. Baxter and I are so looking forward to meeting your parents."

Daria finally found her tongue. "I asked my mother to save a place for you right next to us."

"That was very thoughtful of you. Boys, help Mariah with our things."

Then Daria noticed the slim, dark figure straightening the contents of a basket. Mariah wore a simple yellow calico dress that hung straight from her tiny waist. Her hair was tied at the back of her neck with a worn blue ribbon. She did not look up even as she lifted the basket out of the carriage.

"I can help," Daria offered.

"Don't be silly," Mrs. Baxter said. "Mariah and the twins can manage perfectly well." She turned to Mariah. "Be sure to keep something for yourself. I don't want you getting ill from hunger and too much sun."

"Yes, ma'am," Mariah said softly. "I set aside a piece of chicken. I don't require much."

"You know you can take as much food as you need. You're skinny as a rail as it is."

Deborah Baxter swooped around and surveyed the meadow dotted with picnickers. "Daria, perhaps you will be kind enough to direct us to your family."

Daria glanced at DJ, who had taken a blanket from the back of the Baxter carriage. He smiled gently. TJ reluctantly picked up a second basket. Daria turned to lead the way across the meadow.

She found her parents alone on their quilt. David was

off looking for baseball players. Her older siblings, Tina and Charles, had gone off with their own friends.

"Mama, Papa," Daria said, "these are the Baxters, the people David and I told you about."

Kevin and Pamela Fisk rose to their feet.

"We're delighted you could join us," Papa said. "Let me help you with your things." He relieved Mariah of her load, then smiled at her. "Hello. I'm Dr. Fisk."

Mariah did not lift her eyes. She nodded silently.

"I think we can manage from here, Mariah," Deborah Baxter said. "Why don't you find some shade to sit in. I'll call you if we need anything."

"Yes, ma'am."

Daria watched as Mariah quietly turned to walk away. Then she looked at her father. Their eyes met.

"There is no need for Mariah to leave," Papa said. "We have plenty of room and plenty of food."

Mrs. Baxter waved one hand. "I assure you, Mariah is content to be alone. She would be quite uncomfortable staying here."

Daria saw Mariah settle under a tree about fifty feet away.

"Can we go find David?" TJ asked.

"Certainly," his mother answered. "I'm eager to meet him."

"When you find him," Daria's mother said, "ask him to come back here."

"Which way should we look?" DJ asked Daria.

Daria pointed. "He went that way."

"Daria, why don't you stay here with us?" her mother said. "Let's get acquainted with our new friends."

"Yes, Mama," Daria said, sighing. Her lower lip hung out just a bit as she watched the Baxter twins scamper off to find David. She dropped to the quilt awkwardly. As the adults lowered themselves more gracefully, her mother gave her a warning look.

"My children tell me that you have only recently come to Cincinnati," Papa said.

"That's correct. We've been here about two weeks," Mr. Baxter answered. "My family has been farming in South Carolina for several generations. Our land holdings are quite extensive, and our cotton crops do well every year."

"Then why have you come north to run a shoe factory?"

Mr. Baxter pressed his lips together. "My brothers and I thought it would be prudent to diversify our business holdings. We are quite certain that there will always be a demand for shoes, so it seemed a wise investment."

"My husband thought about purchasing a factory in New Hampshire," Mrs. Baxter said, "but I preferred Cincinnati. It is much closer to the South and like the South in many ways. I think we will feel more at home here."

"Managing a shoe factory will be quite different from farming cotton," Mama observed.

"Yes, of course," Mr. Baxter answered. "Naturally the labor costs are much higher here."

"A day's work is worth a day's pay," Papa remarked.

A knot formed in Daria's stomach.

"A good slave can be quite expensive," Mr. Baxter replied, "but I do believe using slaves is still more efficient than paying daily wages. We take care of our people. They are not unhappy."

Daria felt the knot tighten in her stomach. Her parents

hated the idea of slavery. Would they be able to sit and eat lunch with people like the Baxters? Daria was glad Charles was not around. He seldom held his tongue, and he had strong opinions about everything—especially slavery.

Papa continued politely. "Some people think that the Southern way of life will change. Perhaps you have come to Cincinnati because you share that view."

"I have always treasured our life in South Carolina," Mr. Baxter replied. "But politics are unpredictable right now. If Abraham Lincoln is elected president, we may find ourselves glad to have a business in the North."

"And do you think Mr. Lincoln will be elected?" Papa asked.

The knot in Daria's stomach tightened some more. Wouldn't it be better to talk about something else? she wondered.

"I do not believe Mr. Lincoln is the leader that this country needs," Mr. Baxter said. "But I am aware that many people in the North, especially Ohio, think quite highly of him."

Papa only nodded. Daria was relieved. She and David had just met TJ and DJ. She wanted to be friends with them. If their parents quarreled over politics, she and David might not be allowed to play with the Baxter twins.

"I don't know what I would do without Mariah," Mrs. Baxter said. "I realized, of course, that we could not bring all of our household help to Cincinnati with us, but I could not possibly think of leaving Mariah behind. She's far too valuable to me. I wouldn't be able to get through the day without her help. Running a household is quite a job."

Mama nodded. "Many families in Cincinnati hire people to come in and help with the work of the house."

"Mariah takes care of so many details for me," Mrs. Baxter continued. "And I know I can trust her completely with the boys. She is even reliable with money. If I send her to the market, she buys what we need and brings me the change."

"It's good to have someone to depend on," Mama said. "My older daughter, Christina, is quite helpful in that way. And, of course, as Daria gets older, she will be of more and more help."

Daria was holding her breath. How much longer could her parents continue this polite conversation without letting their true feelings explode?

Just then the three boys thundered up to the quilts and collapsed in a heap. Tina was close behind them.

"Tina, come and meet the Baxters," Mama said. "No doubt you have heard the twins talking about their boys."

"Yes, I have," Tina said enthusiastically. "I'm very pleased to meet you."

"When do we eat?" David wanted to know.

"David, why don't you say hello to Mr. and Mrs. Baxter?" Papa prodded his youngest son.

David sat up and wiped his grubby hands on his trouser legs. "I'm glad to meet you. And I'm glad you moved here. I really like TJ and DJ."

Mr. Baxter chuckled. "I can see that, and I believe the feeling is mutual."

David grinned at the Baxter twins.

"Did you find enough players?" Daria asked.

"We have seventeen," David answered. "We just need to find one more player to have real teams, nine on each team."

"What position will I play?" Daria asked.

"No position," David said. "We don't need girls today. This is going to be a real game."

"But you just said you need one more person. Why won't you let me play?"

"Let her play," DJ urged. "With a little bit of practice, she might make a decent outfielder."

"But she's a girl!"

"So what?" Daria raised her voice.

"Children, children," Mama said in her most soothing voice. "Must you quarrel? I'm sure we can find an answer that makes everybody happy."

Daria stared at David. David stared at Daria.

"Let her play, David," DJ repeated. "It will save us from having to look for another player."

David rolled over onto his stomach. "Oh, all right. But only in the outfield."

Daria grinned. Mama sighed. Mrs. Baxter chuckled.

"DJ is used to playing with a girl," Mrs. Baxter explained, "because Mariah has played ball with the boys since they were small."

Daria turned to look at Mariah, still sitting under a tree. She had a small bundle in her lap—the one piece of chicken she had allowed herself.

Tina followed Daria's gaze. "Is that Mariah over there?" she asked quietly.

Daria nodded.

"Perhaps I'll go say hello."

Tina slipped away before Daria could say anything else.

"I'm hungry," TJ said. "Can we eat now?"

CHAPTER 4

Plans for a Team

TJ whacked the ball on the second pitch that his brother threw. As soon as Daria heard the crack of the bat, she lost hope that she would be able to catch that ball. But she was determined to try. She was not going to give David any reason to think she was not playing just as hard as DJ or TJ, or even David himself.

Daria had played hard at the church picnic game—and her team had won. David, who was on the losing team, refused to talk about the game afterward. But he stopped complaining about girls playing baseball.

The two sets of twins were now playing baseball every day except Sunday. For more than a week, they had met on the school lot each afternoon. DJ and Daria teamed up against TJ and David. And as much as David hated to admit it, the teams were fairly even. The Daria and DJ duo scored just as many runs as David and TJ together.

Daria ran into right field in pursuit of TJ's ball. It was sailing high and deep, and she lost it in the sun. When she finally focused on it again, she realized she had drifted too far back. She stretched out her arms as far as she could and dived for the ball. But she was not close enough. The ball plopped to the ground six inches out of her reach. In one smooth motion, she scooped it up and hurled it toward DJ, who was waiting at second base. They held TJ to a double, but David scored on the hit. Now the score was six to three. David and TJ were ahead.

"You gotta move faster than that!" David shouted at his sister as she brushed the dirt off her pinafore. The ruffle was tearing loose on one side.

David tapped his bat on the home plate made from a broken fence board. Spreading his feet shoulder-width apart, he took up his batting position.

From the infield, DJ turned and signaled that Daria should come in to talk. She trotted in. DJ tossed the ball from one hand to the other as he spoke.

"I think David has figured out my pitches," he said. "I'm not as good a hurler as TJ."

"He knows you can't throw it as fast as TJ, so you have to do something else," Daria said. "Throw it low, around his knees. Maybe he'll lose his sense of timing."

DJ nodded. "You be ready for a line drive. Stay in mid-field."

Daria returned to the outfield, but not too far out this time. She bent over and put her hands on her knees as she studied David. She knew that look in his face. He was confident he was going to smack the ball right over her head. Daria and DJ could not let him do that. They only needed one more out, and they would get a turn to bat and try to even up the score. Daria glared back at David. She wanted him to know she intended to stop him. This time the ball was not going to get away from her.

DJ wound his arm backward in three complete circles and let the ball fly. David shook his head and did not swing. The ball slapped the fence behind him. David picked up the ball and lobbed it back to DJ.

DJ got ready for the next pitch. It was a perfect pitch, straight and fast and low. David swung and missed. The ball clattered against the fence. One strike.

Startled, David took an extra few seconds to toss the ball back to the hurler.

TJ took a lead off second base, as if he was sure David would hit a home run with the next pitch.

DJ threw again. David missed again. Strike two.

In the outfield, Daria cheered. David scowled and took up his position again.

DJ took a long time getting ready for the next pitch. When he finally threw it, David had grown impatient and did not swing well. He missed a perfect pitch by several inches. This was the third strike and the third out.

Daria cheered some more as she trotted in from the outfield. She and DJ were down by three runs, but if they got some good hits, they could make that up and maybe even get ahead.

"Hey, David!" a voice shouted. "Why are you playing baseball with a girl?"

David, Daria, and the Baxter twins looked to see four boys climbing the wooden fence behind home plate.

"She's not a girl. She's my sister," David said. "Besides, it's not a real game. We only have two players on a team."

Tad Leland, Hans Schmidt, Peter Wyeth, and Lars Johnson examined the field.

"Do you play a lot?" Tad asked.

"Every day," David said. "Hey, why don't you play with us? Then we could have four on a team."

TJ and DJ quickly agreed. "That would be much more fun. We'd be able to work on our defense better."

"Hans and Peter," David said, "you go play on DJ and Daria's team. Lars and Tad, you play with TJ and me."

"Who is winning?" Hans asked suspiciously.

"We are," TJ answered.

"Then I want to be on your team," Hans said.

"Never mind," David said. "We'll start over. Your team can strike first."

TJ took his position in the hurler's spot, which was really just a worn area in the grass. David, Peter, and Lars spread themselves behind him around the field.

"Okay," DJ said to his team, "we have to decide who should strike first. I think Daria should go first. She can try to get on first base, then we'll try to move her around the bases." He handed a bat to Daria.

Daria faced off against TJ. When it came to pitching, TJ took no pity on anyone. He could throw the ball fast and straight every time. Many times, the ball hit the fence behind her before Daria even got a good look at it.

"Let's go, Daria," DJ said, clapping his hands. "Let's get a hit."

The first pitch whizzed by. Daria swung hard, but she hardly even saw the ball.

"That's okay," DJ said. "You'll get a good look at the next one."

The second pitch whizzed by. Two strikes.

Daria looked over at DJ for encouragement, but he did not say anything this time.

She planted her feet solidly and got ready for the next pitch. She fixed her eyes on the ball while TJ was standing still. She hardly dared to blink. When the pitch came, she was ready. She swung as hard as she could.

Instead of the crack she had hoped to hear, Daria heard only a knicking sound. She had not hit a home run, but she had hit the ball. It was dribbling through the infield. Dropping her bat, she ran as fast as she could toward the first base stump. Racing to the base, she almost collided with Tad, who had scrambled for the ball. But she got to the base first, and Tad had not been able to tag her.

She let out a sigh of relief. She had done her job. She had gotten to first base. Now it was up to the others on the team to push her around the bases.

DJ got a base hit, and Daria ran all the way to third base before Lars had thrown the ball back to the infield. Hans struck out on three straight pitches. He was not used to TJ's pitching.

Peter stepped up to the plate. If he could get a hit, Daria could score. But he was not used to TJ's pitching, either, so Daria was not too confident. As TJ got ready to throw the pitch, she took a few steps off third base.

To her utter surprise, Peter smacked the first pitch. The ball sailed high and far—farther than anyone on David's team expected. By the time David had recovered the ball and thrown it in to TJ, Daria had scored, with DJ and Peter circling the bases behind her. It was three runs to nothing.

It was Daria's turn to take up the bat again. But this time, she struck out. DJ did not do much better. He hit the ball, but he hit it straight at Lars, who easily caught it.

Their half of the inning was over. But they had scored three runs. Daria thought they had done well.

As David's team came in from the field, TJ signaled that he wanted to talk to everyone.

"You guys did pretty well," he said. "I think we could have a good baseball team."

"That's a great idea!" David said. "We'll find a few more kids, form a team, and try to find other teams to play."

"That's exactly what I was thinking," TJ said.

"Jimmy Smith is a pretty good striker," David said, leaning on his bat. "We could ask him. And his brother might want to play, too."

"Who do you know that can hurl?" TJ asked. "We need good hurlers, too, and some kids who can really throw from the outfield."

"Jake Zappiro is probably the best player in the whole school," David said. "He has to help his parents in their store a lot, but I think we could convince him to join the team."

"Can he throw?" TJ asked.

"He's the best striker there is," David said. "What else do we need?"

"We need someone who can throw," TJ insisted. "You can't have a good baseball team made up of just batters. We need good fielders."

"I'm a good striker," Hans said.

"You struck out on three pitches," Lars reminded him.

"But that doesn't happen every time!" Hans protested. "Wait until you see what it's like to try to hit the balls DJ throws."

"TJ is the hurler," David said, "not DJ."

"How can you tell them apart?" Hans asked. He looked from one identical twin to the other, confused.

"Just remember that TJ is the great hurler."

"And what if he's not hurling?"

"Never mind. You'll figure them out. The important thing is we're going to have a baseball team. If we find the right strikers, we'll be the best there is." David glanced at TJ. "And we'll look for some throwers, too."

"Let's put up signs and see who wants to play," TJ suggested.

"No, no," David said, shaking his head. "We want to pick the players carefully." He looked at the group gathered around him. "All of you guys can play if you want to. But anybody else has to try out for the team."

TJ squinted his eyes and crossed his arms across his chest. Daria understood exactly why. It had been TJ's idea to start a baseball team. Now David was taking over. David had taken over lots of ideas that had started with Daria. She was used to it. But TJ was not.

"Let's get back to the game," Daria said. "We can talk

40

about the team later."

TJ tossed the ball to his twin. "Try to put some speed on it," he said. "Don't make it so easy for us this time."

Daria walked out to her spot in the outfield. Hans followed her, while Peter stayed at shortstop, and DJ got ready to pitch. Having a baseball team was a great idea. But Daria had a funny feeling about all of this.

CHAPTER 5

Tina's Plan

"Daria, stand still!" Mama pleaded. She tugged a brush through her daughter's scraggly reddish brown hair. "We must get your hair under control before we can go to the meeting."

"But I don't want to go to the meeting!" Daria protested. "It will be boring."

"You cannot be sure about that. You've never been to one of these committee meetings before."

"Will there be any other girls my age there?"

Mama sighed. "I don't know. Occasionally some of the women bring their children. But that doesn't matter. I want you to go."

"But why? There's a baseball practice today."

"I think it is wonderful that you and David have found

something to do together," Mama said as she set the brush down on the dresser. "But you are becoming a young lady. You cannot spend all your time playing baseball."

Daria crossed her arms across the front of her pinafore and pouted.

"I want you to appreciate how fortunate you are," Mama said. "Hundreds of children in this very city have lost their parents or have been left behind by their parents. They do not live in fine houses like ours. They live in an old building that could burn down at any moment. They share a bedroom with so many children that there is hardly space to walk across the room."

"Yes, Mama," Daria muttered.

"Besides, you haven't seen your cousin Meg in a long time."

"She's too busy to see me." Daria liked Meg, but Meg was twenty-eight years old and worked as a nurse. She had no time for ten-year-old girls.

"This is your opportunity to see her and to share one of her interests."

"But David gets to play baseball."

"I know this doesn't seem fair to you," Pamela said. "But I can't very well take David to a meeting of the Women's Committee for Social Concerns. He'll have to learn about these things another way."

Nineteen-year-old Tina appeared in the doorway. "Mama, Meg is waiting in the carriage outside. Shall I ask her to come in?"

"No, we must go," Mama said. "Daria is ready." She put the brush down on Daria's dresser.

In the carriage, Daria huddled to one side, still pouting.

At that very moment, David and TJ and DJ and all the other boys were playing baseball. And she was stuck with her Sunday dress and bows in her hair, on her way to a meeting she did not want to go to. At suppertime she was going to tell about every detail of the meeting and make David listen to every word.

"Are you ready for the meeting?" Meg asked Tina. She nudged the horse forward.

"I think so," Tina said. "I have some specific ideas I want to suggest."

"Good. I hope we can come up with a good plan to do something to help the orphans."

"Agreeing on a plan will not be easy," Mama warned. "Not everyone on the committee understands the real problems."

They arrived at the church. Meg hitched the horse, and the four of them entered the parish hall. About fifteen wooden chairs stood in a circle. Against one wall of the room was a bowl of punch and a tray of cookies. Daria headed over to the table.

"Just one cookie!" her mother warned.

Daria chose the sugar cookie that looked the biggest, then went to sit next to her mother. Meg sat on the other side of her. Tina, to her surprise, stood across the circle from them.

"Isn't Tina going to sit with us?" Daria asked.

"She's in charge of the meeting," her mother answered.

"She is?"

Daria looked around. Tina was the youngest person in the room, except for Daria. Mrs. Adams was there, and Mrs. Wyeth. Miss Kronk sat sipping punch next to her mother,

Mrs. Kronk, who Daria thought must be at least ninety years old. Mrs. Collier, Mrs. Smith, and Miss Barnett made up the rest of the Methodist Women's Committee for Social Concerns.

"Perhaps we should begin," Tina said confidently. "Thank you, Mrs. Collier, for the punch and cookies. Please help yourselves to the refreshments as we are talking. Today we want to discuss some practical solutions to the growing number of orphans in Cincinnati. For instance, what can we do to encourage people to adopt orphans? Children need homes. We must help as many of them as possible to get into real homes, loving homes, with parents."

"I think we have to find some way to stop the number of orphans from getting any larger," said Mrs. Adams. "Many of those children are not really orphans. They have parents, but they have simply been abandoned. The parents know there is an orphanage their children can go to. So when they grow tired of the responsibility of being a parent, they leave their children behind."

"Perhaps that is true in some cases," Tina said carefully, "but we must be careful not to punish the children for the mistakes their parents made."

Daria eyed the refreshment table and wondered if it would really be all right to get up and help herself to the refreshments, as Tina had said. She twisted her head around to see if anyone else had punch. The crinoline petticoat under her dress rustled as she moved.

"Shhh!" her mother said. Daria obediently turned around to face forward. But she still wanted punch. She started swinging her feet beneath her chair.

Her mother nudged her with her elbow and leaned over

to whisper in Daria's ears. "Sit still. You are old enough to care about what happens to these children."

Daria looked at Tina again.

"I believe we must find practical solutions that focus on the problems that the children have," Tina said. "If we can also find a way to stop the increasing number of children who are left at the orphanage, that would be wonderful as well. But my concern is for the children."

"Someone has to take responsibility for this problem," Miss Kronk said. "It will not stop until someone takes responsibility."

"I agree that we must try to keep people from leaving their children at the orphanage," Tina said patiently. "For today, I would like for us to think about what we can do for the children themselves."

"Do you have some suggestions?" Mrs. Smith asked.

"Yes, I do. I believe the first thing we should do is begin a clothing drive. Many of the clothes I've seen the children wearing are hardly more than rags. I think they deserve something new. So we could sew for them."

"I'm already sewing clothes for. . .well, you know, other people who need them just as badly," Mrs. Wyeth said. "I don't believe I can sew any more or any faster."

Daria wondered what Mrs. Wyeth was talking about. But Tina nodded her understanding.

"Thank you, Mrs. Wyeth. I know everyone appreciates your fine work." She turned to the group. "What about some of the rest of you? Can any of you spare some time to sew? Or do you have used clothing that is still in good condition? Children often outgrow clothes quickly, before the clothes wear out."

"I might have a few things that Jimmy can't wear anymore," Mrs. Smith said.

"What about food?" Tina said. "All of us have preserves in our pantries and cellars. Perhaps we could spare something for the children. I know some of you have vegetable gardens that produce more than you can possibly eat. This is September—harvest time. Can we share our abundance with the children?"

Daria listened intently to Tina. Her brother Charles was excited about railroads. David loved baseball. Until now, Daria had not realized that Tina cared so deeply about anything, except perhaps for Enoch Stevenson, who was courting Tina. Daria thought Tina had some good ideas. She liked the idea of doing something, not simply talking about the problem.

"This problem is much bigger than we are," Miss Barnett said. "Even if we were all to clean out our closets and pantries and adopt some children, there would still be many, many more children left at the orphanage. Can we really make any difference by what we are doing?"

"That's exactly my point," Mrs. Adams said emphatically. "We can collect clothes and preserves, but that does not solve the problem. The children will keep coming. The more attractive we make it to be in an orphanage, the more children will end up there."

"I agree with Tina," Meg said. "We must not let the children suffer because of the mistakes their parents have made. The Lord knows what the problems are. Only God can give the answers. But we must do what God asks us to do. And with God's help, we can do what we must do."

"I don't like to see children in orphanages any more than

I like to see slaves in bondage," Mrs. Wyeth said. "Of course I want to help. But it's difficult to know what to do."

"Why do you sew for. . .for the less fortunate?" Meg asked Mrs. Wyeth.

"I suppose I do it because I can do it. It's a small contribution to a cause that I believe in."

"That is all that God asks of us," Meg said, "to do what we can."

"And when we think we can't," Tina said, "then God helps even more."

Daria had not thought about the baseball practice she was missing for quite a while now. She had not even thought about the refreshment table and the cookies that no one seemed to be eating. Why hadn't she ever noticed that Tina was so interested in the orphanages of Cincinnati? Daria wondered. Jimmy Smith and Peter Wyeth were playing baseball at that very moment, while their mothers sat in a parish hall talking about helping the orphans. Did they know their mothers cared about things like that?

"If you would like to contribute clothing or food for the orphanage," Tina said, "please speak to me after the meeting. I will be glad to make the arrangements. I would like to mention one more idea. I have visited the orphanage a few times, but I have not seen anything but the director's office and a few of the children. I plan to take a tour of the entire building to determine what other needs they may have. Would any of you be willing to come with me?"

Daria looked around the room at the shocked faces.

"There may be diseases in that old building," Mrs. Adams said suspiciously.

"If there are, we must wipe them out," Tina said.

"Some of those children are like wild animals," Miss Barnett said. "We could be putting ourselves in danger."

"They are just children," Tina said. "If they act like animals, it is because they have never known a parent's love."

Daria had never been to the orphanage before, but from the stories she had heard, it did not sound like a very nice place to go. She had trouble imagining the women on the committee driving up to the orphanage in their carriages and entering the building in their fine dresses.

"I intend to accompany my daughter on her visit to the orphanage," Mama said. Daria recognized the tone in her mother's voice. Mama had made up her mind, and nothing would change it.

"Of course, I will go with you as well," Meg said.

"Thank you, Mama. Thank you, Meg." Tina looked around the room, hoping for more responses.

"Perhaps I would be free to accompany you as well," Mrs. Wyeth finally said. "As you say, they are just children. What do we have to fear?"

No one else spoke. After a few minutes of silence, Tina said, "Very well then. I shall make the arrangements and contact those of you who wish to participate. Meg, would you please say a word of prayer before we close our meeting?"

All the heads in the room bowed, even those with the largest hats. Daria bowed her head and squeezed her eyes shut. But she hardly heard a word Meg said. She could not stop thinking about Tina, only nineteen years old, trying to organize all these older women into action—to stop talking and start doing.

CHAPTER 6

A Bad Practice

The school bell did not ring soon enough for Daria—or for David and the Baxter twins. As soon as class was dismissed on that afternoon in the middle of September, both sets of twins bolted from the building and darted to the baseball field.

The beginning of a new school year had shortened their daily practices. Now they had to wait until after school to begin and had to stop in time for supper. But it had not affected their enthusiasm for playing baseball. TJ and David had recruited several new players. Now they had more than the nine players they needed for a team. They had enough players to make substitutions or to allow for days when some of them could not come to practice.

David found five other teams that they could play against. All the teams had started out like theirs—boys playing together in empty lots or even in the streets. David had challenged every one of the informal groups to a game, and that is how they all became teams.

All the boys on her team were running ahead of Daria out of the school building. Her mother's talks about being more ladylike had persuaded Daria that she had to act like a lady—until she got to the baseball field. Then she intended to be just as tough and strong as any of the boys. Daria was one of the best outfielders that the team had. Even David had to admit that none of the boys could throw a ball in from midfield as well as Daria could.

When she got to the first-base stump, Daria threw down her schoolbooks and lunch pail in the heap with all the others. The team had their first game the next day. This practice was an important one.

She saw David and TJ sitting in the grass together. David had a piece of paper in his hand and was pointing to different spots on the page. Daria shuffled through the grass until she could hear what they were talking about.

"Hans has a lot of strength," David said, "but his swing is uneven. He needs to work on that."

"He has a good arm, though," TJ said. "When he plays shortstop, he throws to first really well."

"But he has to learn to strike better. Now, Tad is a great striker. I don't think we have to worry about him."

"Haven't you noticed that he misses every fly ball that comes his way?" TJ said. "We need to hit him some flies during practice so he can learn to get under them and catch them."

David shrugged his shoulders. "Whatever. As long as he can hit." He pointed to another name on the list. "What about Peter?"

"I think Peter could learn to hurl," TJ said.

"But you're great at hurling," David said. "Why do we need Peter to throw?"

"I don't have to hurl every game. I think Peter would like to do it."

"We can't take the chance," David said. "We know we can count on you. Everybody you throw to has trouble with your fastball."

"But maybe Peter can hurl well, too."

David shook his head. "No, we need Peter on third base. And he's a good striker."

Daria knew her twin well enough to know that TJ would not be able to make David change his mind. A lot of people thought Daria was stubborn. And maybe she was. But the older they got, the more stubborn David got. Once he made up his mind, that was it. Tina said it was because he had had so much practice quarreling with Daria when they were little.

"What are they talking about?" DJ walked up and stood next to Daria.

"David has a list of who is good at striking," Daria said.

"And I suppose TJ is talking about who is good at throwing," DJ said. They had both heard conversations like this before.

"Exactly," Daria said. "I have a funny feeling that this is not going to be a good practice."

David stood up and clapped his hands. "Okay, everyone, gather around and let's get started. Tomorrow is our first real game, and we have to be ready for it. I think we should break into two squads and have a practice game. Let's concentrate on getting hits. Let's keep the other team running tomorrow, tire them out."

"David," TJ said, "I think we should drill some skills for a few minutes first."

"Drill some skills?"

"Yes. Practice catching. Practice throwing the ball in from the outfield. Practice fielding ground balls. That kind of stuff."

"We'll get to do that if we just play a game," David responded.

"But we need to practice doing those things so we can do them well in a game."

"We don't have much time before players have to start going home for supper. If we spend our time drilling, we won't have time for a real game."

"Playing a game today doesn't matter," TJ insisted. "What matters is practicing skills so we'll be ready for tomorrow."

"I want everyone to have the feel of a real game," David said. "We need to make sure everyone knows the rules and what to do in different situations."

"Make up your minds, you guys," Hans said. "We're just wasting time." He threw a ball up in the air. He missed it when it came back down.

David pulled TJ away from the group. They bent their heads together, one brown, one blond, and whispered.

Daria could not hear what they were saying. But she

could see the expressions on their faces. TJ was getting redder and redder.

"Is that what he looks like when he's mad?" she asked DJ.

"Yes, he's mad, all right," DJ said.

"What do you think they're saying?"

"If I know TJ, he's saying exactly what he thinks."

"David, too."

They fell silent for a moment, watching their brothers in a private huddle.

"How did they end up in charge of the team instead of us?" Daria wondered aloud.

"I don't know," DJ said. "But I think we're stuck with them now."

David and TJ broke apart.

"Okay, we've discussed it," David announced, "and we've decided that we will play a game today. Here are the teams. Hans, Peter, DJ, Daria, Jake, Jimmy, and Tad will be one team. Peter will hurl and Jake will catch behind. TJ, Lars, Conrad, Gerald, Patrick, and I will be the other team. TJ will hurl and Conrad will be behind."

Daria looked at TJ. His pointed chin jutted out a bit more than usual, but he did not say anything.

The game began. Daria's team batted first, with Jake leading off. After tipping a ball foul, he swung at and missed the next two pitches. One out.

Jimmy was up next. Daria did not really expect he would get on base. He usually hit the ball, but often it was a ground ball that did not make it out of the infield.

Jimmy let the first pitch go by. He swung at the second one and missed. He swung at the third pitch and missed again. Now he had two strikes. Jimmy got ready for the next pitch. TJ wound up and threw. It was a good pitch, headed right over the center of the plate but a little bit low. When Jimmy swung, he grazed the top of the ball with the bat, knocking it into the infield. He had done exactly what Daria had feared he would do. Certain Jimmy would be tagged or thrown out, she turned to see who would bat next.

"Get it, get it!" someone shouted. Daria turned back to the field. Gerald, playing second base, had let Jimmy's ground ball roll past him into right field. There it stopped in the grass, far away from any of the other players.

As David's teammates scrambled to get the ball, Gerald, who was a fast runner, scrambled to first base safely.

Hans came up to bat next. Daria kept one eye on Gerald. As TJ got ready for the next pitch, Gerald drifted away from first base—too far, Daria thought. But as soon as TJ let go of the ball, Gerald put his head down and started running.

Hans swung and missed. The ball smacked into Conrad's hands. Seeing Gerald headed for second base, Conrad leaped to feet and hurled the ball toward David at second.

The throw was wide—it went closer to third base than second—and sailed into left field.

Gerald kept running. He easily rounded second and headed for third. His entire team, including Daria, was cheering him on and waving him toward home plate.

By the time David's team had the ball under control, Gerald had scored the first run of the game. Hans was still at bat with only one strike.

"Gerald stole second base. Stealing is against the 1845 Knickerbocker rules," Conrad protested.

"Then why did you try to throw him out?" Hans challenged.

"Let's just get back to the game," TJ said.

Frustrated, TJ got ready to pitch once again. Hans swung at the next pitch and put all his weight into the swing. The ball flew high into center field, where Lars waited for it. It should have been an easy catch. But Lars had his hands too far apart. The ball dropped between them, rolled through his legs, and stopped behind him. He turned in circles three times trying to find it. In the meantime, Hans had run to second base.

It was Daria's turn to bat.

"You can do it," DJ said. "Just get a base hit, and Hans can score."

Daria pressed her lips together and faced TJ. Looking at him was so much like looking at DJ that she had to remind herself of the power of TJ's pitch.

The first pitch smacked into Conrad's hands. He jumped up, ready to throw if Hans tried to run. Hans stayed on second base.

Daria swung at the next pitch, tipping it foul. Ball one, strike one.

"Concentrate, Daria!" DJ called. "You can do it."

Daria bit her bottom lip as she tried to focus. The pitch came. She swung. She hit the ball—not hard, but she had hit it. She dashed toward first base, even though she knew TJ would easily pick up the ball and throw her out. TJ's throw was right on target. And Patrick caught it. But then he dropped it. Hans rounded third and headed for home, scoring easily while Patrick tried to recover the ball from the bushes. Daria ran toward second.

TJ stood in the hurler's spot with his hands on his hips. "Don't you see, David? We're not ready for a game. We need to practice our defensive skills. Jimmy's ground ball should never have gotten out of the infield. Conrad should have been able to throw that ball straight to you. Patrick should have caught that easy toss. They just scored two runs because of our mistakes."

Everyone stood and watched TJ challenge David.

"We're going to set up drill stations," TJ said calmly to everyone. "Conrad, if you're going to be the team catcher, you have to learn to throw on target. I'll practice with you."

"We're in the middle of a game!" David protested.

"Yeah!" Jake said. "Our team didn't get a chance to strike yet."

"We'll never get a chance to strike in tomorrow's game if we don't do something about our fielding. They'll have us running all over the field until we drop from exhaustion. We need someone to hit the ball, and the rest of you practice fielding. We can do striking practice a few at a time. Peter can help throw."

Surprised at TJ's outburst, the other players slowly began moving in several directions, following his instructions.

DJ and Daria looked at each other, each torn by their loyalties to their own twin.

David stood at second base for a long time, scowling. Finally he moved toward third base and said, "I'll hit flies. But in a half hour, we start batting practice." Several players followed David to an open space and he began hitting the ball, over and over.

TJ concentrated on coaching Conrad to throw the ball better. He never looked at David.

DJ and Daria looked at each other and shrugged. Then they followed David to the outfield.

CHAPTER 7

The First Game

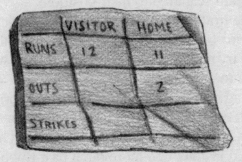

TJ bent over, put his hands on his knees, and looked somberly at his teammates. It was their first game, and things weren't going well.

"This striker has already gotten two hits," he said. "We're behind by one run, so we have to make sure he does not get on base."

Daria glanced at the striker, Robby Bell. He was in her grade at school. He hated to lose even a spelling bee or a reading contest. Robby tapped the bat on the ground and glowered at his opponents, daring them to challenge him.

"Daria, don't go out as far as you usually do," TJ instructed. "He hits the ball high, but not real far. You should be able to get under it."

"I'll do my best."

"We can't afford any mistakes now," TJ warned the whole team.

"Don't forget," David said, "we still have a turn to bat. We'll get back at them."

TJ shook his head. "We can't count on that. We have to get this guy out."

The team scattered to their positions.

As she trotted back out to midfield, Daria scanned the sky. Before beginning their first game, both teams had agreed to try to play five innings. By then, it would be getting close to suppertime. It was already late. The first two innings had been very long, with a lot of scoring. Now the score was twelve to eleven, and their team was losing.

Robby Bell had two strikes, and his team had two outs. If TJ could just get one more pitch past Robby, the twins' team might have a chance.

TJ was ready to throw. He cranked his arm around and let go of one of the fastest pitches he had ever thrown. It whizzed past Robby, who swung very hard, but very late. The ball smacked into the catcher's waiting hands. Robby lost his balance and tumbled to the ground.

David whooped like a wild elephant and rushed from second base toward home plate. Hans, Peter, Conrad, and the others were all behind him, hollering just as loudly.

"All right, let's huddle," David said. He gathered the team around him. "Here's what we need to do. It's important that the first striker get on base. Lars, that's you. Do whatever you have to do to get on base."

"Right," agreed Lars.

"Then try to steal second," David said.

"I'm not so sure about that," TJ said. "Lars may not be fast enough. They have some good throwers on their team."

"We have to steal second," insisted David, "so that there's no chance of a double play when DJ comes up to bat."

"Isn't stealing against the rules?" Lars asked. "That's what Conrad said yesterday."

"Don't pay any attention to Conrad," David said. "This is a good plan."

"This is our last chance, David," TJ protested, "and we're behind. We can't take chances."

"We have to take chances, or we have no hope of winning."

"Don't worry, I can do it," Lars said, and he reached for a bat.

"Just get on base," TJ said.

The rest of the team stepped back and let Lars step up to the plate. Daria's stomach churned a little bit. Lars was a loyal player. He came to every practice, and he did not make too many mistakes. But he struck out a lot.

The first pitch came, and Lars swung. The bat whooshed through empty air.

David clapped his hands several times and called out, "It's all right, Lars. That's only the first throw. You'll get the next one."

Lars moved slightly closer to the plate and took his stance. This time he caught the edge of the ball and knocked it foul. Strike two. Daria swallowed hard. It looked like Lars would strike out again. She looked away.

Then she heard the sharp crack. Lars had hit the next pitch! It was not a hard hit, but it was a good connection. The ball lobbed over the pitcher's head. Lars took off for first base.

When the ball landed, it bounced a few times before the player at second base scooped it up. The ball never made it out of the infield. Lars was easily thrown out before he reached first base.

Out number one. Only two more chances.

DJ picked up his favorite bat. He looked confident to Daria, and she felt confident, too. If he could hit her on the head with a ball while she sat under a tree across a field, he could get a base hit now.

The first throw came. It looked like a good one to Daria. She would have swung. But DJ did not. Instead, he took a step away from the plate.

"That was a great pitch!" David roared. "What are you waiting for?"

DJ ignored David and focused on the hurler again. He held the bat out in front of him, ready to meet the ball.

Once again he let the pitch go past him. Daria clutched her skirt in her fist. Why was he letting such good pitches go by?

The third pitch came. This time DJ swung. He hit a straight, hard line drive into left field. DJ had passed first base and was on his way to second before the left fielder even got to the ball. As he triumphantly came to a standing stop at second base, the rest of his team whooped and hollered.

"Great job, DJ!"

"You sure know your pitches!"

"Good running!"

David was ecstatic. There was only one out, and they had a runner at second base. With no one on first base, there was no chance of a double play.

"Okay, Conrad, it's your turn," David said as he rubbed his hands on his cotton trousers. "A good base hit will score DJ, and we'll be tied."

Conrad swung the bat four or five times to show he was ready.

"Keep the bat straight," David said, demonstrating with his own bat. "Nice and even."

Conrad was far too impatient to wait for the perfect pitch. He swung at the first one and missed. Strike one.

Unruffled, he got back into position and waited for the next pitch. He swung again. This time he hit the ball.

Daria did not know what to watch. At the sound of the bat striking the ball, DJ had darted toward third base. Conrad was hustling to first. The ball headed toward the second baseman, who was standing between first and second. He tossed the ball to the player at first, and Conrad was out. But DJ was now on third base.

It was Daria's turn. With two outs and the tying run on third base, the pressure was on. She wet her lips as she picked up a bat.

"Just a minute." David stopped her. "I think we should make a substitution."

As nervous as she was, Daria wanted to bat. If she was a real member of the team, she was not going to back out when the pressure was on.

"No, I want to do it," Daria said. She stared her twin in the eyes.

"Tad has not played at all today," David said.

"That's because he didn't get here until the third inning," Daria said. "I've been playing hard the whole game. I deserve to strike."

"You're tired. We need a fresh player."

"You didn't say that for Lars or DJ or Conrad," Daria pointed out. "You're just saying that because I'm a girl."

David kicked the dirt. "Aw, come on, Daria, let Tad bat."

"No!" Daria would discuss it no further. She took her place at the plate, set her feet, set her jaw, and stared at the pitcher.

Daria was not the kind of striker that DJ was, but she was not bad, either. She almost always got on base. All she had to do was get a base hit so DJ could score. Then the pressure would be on someone else to get a hit so she could advance.

She decided to try DJ's strategy. When the first throw came, she thought it was too low. She let it go by.

David groaned.

"That was a perfect pitch!" he shouted. "When you see a good pitch, swing!"

Daria paid no attention. She looked around the infield as the ball was thrown back to the hurler. Her brown eyes locked onto DJ's gray eyes at third base. DJ nodded ever so slightly.

With her forearm, Daria brushed back the loose hair falling into her eyes and raised the bat again.

The next pitch was a little too high. If she reached for it, she would knock it foul. She let it pass.

David groaned again.

The third throw was the one she had been waiting for. As soon as it left the hurler's hand, Daria knew this was the ball for her. Sucking in her bottom lip and squinting slightly, she swung as hard and straight as she could.

The bat hit the ball with a crack. She pushed the bat all the way around and saw the ball start to sail. It went up and out, farther than any ball in the game so far. Even DJ had not had such a good hit.

Her entire team was on their feet, cheering wildly. As DJ watched the ball, he started running toward home.

Daria had never seen such a beautiful hit. She could not believe it was hers! The ball almost seemed to float on its way out to left field.

"Run, Daria, run!" her teammates shouted.

She started to run. But she kept one eye on the ball. Its arc was coming down now, and it looked like it was going to be right up against the wooden fence at the back of the schoolyard—a home run. DJ had crossed the plate. The score was tied. All Daria had to do was run around the bases, tag home plate, and the game would be theirs.

In her excitement, she hardly noticed Robby Bell in left field running furiously toward the fence. It seemed impossible that he could catch that ball.

Daria rounded first base and headed toward second. She ran with her head turned toward center field. Her steps slowed.

Robby Bell leaped, stretched out one hand, and caught her beautiful fly ball, her wonderful, game-winning home run. She stopped midway to second base. Out number three. The game was over. Their team had lost.

Daria could not even look up. She walked toward her teammates with her head hanging low. Maybe she should have let Tad strike, she thought. Then she would not be responsible for losing the game.

DJ trotted alongside her and put one hand on her shoulder. "That was a great hit, Daria. And it was a great catch. You have nothing to be ashamed about."

"A few more feet, even a few more inches, and we would have won the game."

"You did your best."

TJ gestured that the team should gather around.

"That was a great hit," he said, "but it was caught. So you see, we can't depend only on good hitting."

"If we had hit better earlier in the game," David said, "it would not have mattered that Daria's hit was caught."

"If we had been fielding better all through the game," TJ said, a little loudly, "Daria would not have been under such pressure to get a hit. They scored a lot of runs they should never have had."

"All you ever talk about is better fielding, better throwing," David said. "I'm getting tired of hearing about it."

"All you ever talk about is getting hits. We got a lot of hits, but what good did it do us?" TJ was turning red in the face, and it was not from the afternoon heat.

"Who do you think you are, bossing me around?" David swiped his fist at the air in front of TJ's face.

DJ and Daria instinctively jumped and grabbed their twins, pulling them farther apart by the elbows.

"This is not the only team in town, you know," TJ said. "It's not even the best team. We lost our first game. I'm a good hurler. I could go play on any team I want."

"I dare you," growled David. "You've spent too much time working on this team. You won't leave us now."

"Just wait and see!"

CHAPTER 8

Helping the Orphans

Daria's disappointment over losing the game was not helped when she got home and discovered that Mama expected her to attend another meeting of the Women's Committee for Social Concerns.

"Mama," she started to protest.

"Daria, that will be all," Mama said in the quiet, but stern voice that meant the matter was settled. "I want you to hear our report on the visit to the orphanage, and I will speak to David myself to insure that he understands that *I* am making you miss this practice."

So that was how Daria found herself the next day following Mama into the parish hall. She saw the same circle of wooden chairs she had seen at the last meeting. But instead of cookies and punch, there was tea and strudel on the refreshment table. Tina and their cousin Meg were just finishing setting out cups and plates. Mrs. Adams was there, and Mrs. Wyeth, Miss Kronk and her ancient mother, Mrs. Kronk, Mrs. Collier, Miss Barnett, and Mrs. Smith.

It was the same group of faces Daria had seen at the last meeting—with one exception. Deborah Baxter sat beside Mrs. Smith, with her great hoop skirt overflowing the chair and draping the floor.

"Why, Daria, my dear," she drawled, "I am so delighted to see you again, and dressed like a proper lady, too."

Daria looked down at her Sunday dress, which she had put on for the meeting, even though it was not Sunday.

Mama nudged her from behind.

"It's nice to see you, too, Mrs. Baxter."

"We're delighted you're here," Mama said. "I was not aware of your interest in the committee."

"Mrs. Smith invited me. She explained that y'all are trying to do something for the poor orphans. Of course, I want to do my part." Mrs. Baxter waved one hand lazily through the air. "Of course, in South Carolina, we were members of a different church, but I don't suppose the Lord will mind if we associate with another type of Christian while we are in the North."

"Do you think God belongs to a particular denomination?" Daria blurted out.

"Hush, Daria," Mama said softly.

"Why, it's perfectly all right," Mrs. Baxter said. "What an amusing question." She laughed and touched the back of her hair, which looked artificially poofed up to Daria. "No, I don't suppose God is a Baptist, a Methodist, or a member of any other church, for that matter."

"I think everyone is here," Tina said brightly from the other side of the circle. "Why don't we begin?"

With her fingertips in Daria's back, Mama nudged her toward a chair.

When everyone was seated, Tina cleared her throat.

"I would like to begin with a report on our visit to the orphanage. My mother accompanied me, along with Meg Allerton, Mrs. Wyeth, and Miss Kronk. Would any of you like to share your impressions?"

"I will," Meg Allerton said.

Daria turned toward her cousin to listen. Tina had urged Daria to visit the orphanage, too, but Daria had not wanted to and Mama had said that it was her decision. She was afraid of what she might see. Now she was not sure she wanted to hear what Meg and the others had to say.

"In my work as a nurse, I have seen a lot of suffering and illness. But I was not prepared for what I saw at the orphanage. The staff there are doing the best they can. I give them credit for making the food stretch to feed all those children. But there is no way they can be true mothers and fathers to the orphans."

"I thought the same thing," Mama said. "When I saw where the children slept—sometimes five or six in a bed or on the floor—I could not help but think of my own four children, each in their own bed with spacious rooms for all their things."

"The children have no toys, no books, nothing to call their own," Miss Kronk added. "It's difficult even to know where to begin."

"That is why we are here today," Tina said. "It is hard

for us to know where to start, but with God's help, we will know where to begin."

Mrs. Wyeth was shaking her head. "Those children were worse off than a lot of slave children. The country is up in arms about whether the new territories should be allowed to have slaves, and we're not taking care of the problems of our own city. If we can begin to treat blacks as people, we can certainly treat these children as people."

Mrs. Baxter cleared her throat loudly. Daria turned to look at her and had a sick feeling in her stomach. Somehow she knew Deborah Baxter was not going to fit into this group.

"I wonder if any of y'all have been to the South?" she asked.

The ladies looked around the room at each other.

Finally, Mrs. Collier said, "I once went to visit a cousin in Kentucky."

"Did you witness any of the wretchedness dear Mrs. Wyeth has referred to?"

"Actually," Mrs. Collier said, "my cousin grew up in Chicago and would never consider owning another human being."

"Am I to understand, then, that you did not see any poor slave children being mistreated?"

"Well, no, I did not."

Mrs. Baxter looked around the room. "And the rest of you have never been South?"

No one spoke. Daria's stomach felt sicker by the minute.

"I feel I must clarify for you that most slaves are well cared for. Our slaves have their own quarters to share with their own families. We even teach some of the children to read so they can be helpful around the house. Why, in all the years that my family has been farming, we have never once had a slave run away. I assure you that our people are quite happy."

"Does she really believe that?" Daria whispered to Mama. "She makes it sound like one big happy family."

"People believe what they want to believe," Mama whispered back hurriedly. "But this is not the time to talk about this. We must find a way to help Tina."

At that moment, Tina jumped up and said loudly, "Perhaps we should have some refreshment before the tea gets cold." In a flash, she was over at the refreshment table and had the teapot in one hand and a tray of strudel in the other. "Daria, won't you please pass the plates around?"

Daria leaped into action. She grabbed a stack of glass plates from the table and made her way around the circle, insisting that every woman take one whether she wanted one or not. Tina followed her, pouring tea and offering strudel.

"Perhaps we can talk as we eat," Mama suggested. "Now that some of us have seen the orphanage, we may have a clearer idea of what the Lord wants us to do."

"I am sure He wants us to do something," Mrs. Collier agreed. "We cannot turn our backs on what we have seen. The need is too great."

"Let's go back to some of the ideas we talked about last time," Tina suggested. Daria thought her older sister looked relieved that the conversation was under control again. "What about gathering some clothing? I think everyone who visited the orphanage would agree that clothing is a genuine need."

The women discussed various ideas, but when the

meeting was over, all they had agreed upon was that they would bring clothes their children had outgrown to October's meeting.

As soon as they were safely in the carriage, Tina let out a huge sigh. "For a minute, there, I was afraid that we wouldn't get anything accomplished today," she confessed. "Mrs. Baxter certainly brings a new set of tensions to our meetings."

"That's true, dear," Mama said, "but the meeting held together and the women were able to set aside their differences."

"But what did we really do?" Daria asked. "We spent most of the afternoon talking, and all that was agreed upon was that we'd have a clothing drive next month. How does that help the orphans this month?"

Tina smiled. "I understand how you feel. Sometimes, like today, I think I can't talk any sense into the ladies at the committee, but that doesn't stop me from doing what I have to do—what I think God wants me to do."

"I'm only ten years old," Daria said. "God doesn't want me to do anything."

"Don't be too sure about that," Tina replied.

Mama smiled gently at Daria. "I understand your impatience," she said. "But as you grow older, you'll begin to understand that even a little progress is better than no progress at all. And who knows? We may discover that God has something for the three of us to do on our own for those little ones."

Mama's words stayed with Daria over the next few days. She understood the idea of God giving them something to do, but she certainly couldn't imagine how He would do it. She didn't know any orphans. Nor did Mama or Tina, as far as Daria knew.

She was thinking about the orphan question Tuesday afternoon while standing in midfield during baseball practice. David was having them practice fielding, and once again, nothing was heading toward either Daria or DJ. TJ stood off to the side, scowling. While he hadn't quit the team yet, he talked about quitting constantly.

Suddenly, Daria heard a little cry. She looked around. All she saw was the boys on the team. Certainly none of them was making such a noise. Had she imagined it? She cocked her head and listened closely. There it was again. It sounded like a baby or a kitten, but where could it be coming from?

"Psst, Daria. Did you hear that noise?" DJ hissed.

"Yes, but what is it?"

"I don't know, but it sounds like it's coming from near the school. Do you want to go investigate?"

Daria gave a quick glance toward David. He was busy hitting grounders to first base and wasn't even looking in their direction. "Sure," she said to DJ. "Let's go."

The two friends headed toward the school building. As they got closer, the noise got louder.

"There it is!" Daria shouted, running toward a basket by the front door of the school. She looked in the basket and stared straight into the blue eyes of a little dark-haired baby. The baby was bundled up in a blanket and had a note pinned to the blanket. Quickly Daria took the note and began to read. "My name is Kathleen. I am three months old. Please take care of me."

Just then the baby turned red and began to cry loudly. As Daria reached down to pick up little Kathleen, she heard David's loud voice.

"What's going on?" her brother yelled angrily. "I thought we were here to have a baseball practice." He was striding from the field toward Daria and DJ.

"We found a baby," DJ yelled back. "Somebody left a baby at the school door."

"Why would somebody do a thing like that?" David asked as he reached the school building.

"There are any number of reasons," Daria said impatiently, thinking of the discussions she'd heard at the two committee meetings. "It really doesn't matter why the baby was left here. The important thing is to help her."

"Why not just take her to an orphanage?" David asked.

Just then Kathleen let loose a piercing cry. Daria rubbed the baby's back and cradled Kathleen against her shoulder. "There, there," she said soothingly to the baby. Then she glared at her twin. "An orphanage would be almost the worst place in the world for this little one. She's hungry and she needs some loving. I'm taking her home—now."

Without waiting to hear David's response, Daria turned on her heel and walked away. As she headed toward home, she wondered, *Was this the special job God had for Tina, Mama, and her?*

By the time Daria reached her home, Kathleen was in full voice.

"Daria, what is all this—" Mama stopped in midsentence. She stared open-mouthed at the screaming baby.

"Mama, this is Kathleen," Daria explained. "She was

left in a basket at the school door, and I found her during practice."

Mama had regained her composure. "The story can wait, Daria. Right now this child obviously needs some milk and probably some other attention, if my nose is correct. Take her into the kitchen while I gather some supplies."

A few minutes later, Kathleen was in clean clothes and was sucking hungrily on the finger tip of an old glove that was filled with warm milk. Tina, who had just returned home, and Daria sat at the kitchen table while Mama rocked and fed the little baby. Everyone was enjoying the silence.

"Now, Daria," Mama said softly. "Why don't you explain everything from the beginning."

Daria quickly told her story and finished by asking, "Mama, couldn't this be the special task you said God might have for us?"

Mama looked at Daria and then at Tina. She smiled. "I'll need to talk with your papa, but you may be right, Daria. You may be right."

CHAPTER 9

What Daria Overheard

Daria put the book down on her bed. She did not remember anything she had read in the last half an hour. In fact, she had not even turned a page in almost fifteen minutes. She would have trouble explaining to her mother in the morning why she had not finished. Both Daria and David were in trouble already.

It was the middle of October, six weeks into the school year. Daria was busy enough helping take care of little Kathleen. Papa and Meg were fairly certain they knew who Kathleen's mother was. They thought she was a woman whose husband had recently disappeared and who was having a hard time finding work so that she could care for herself and her baby.

While Meg and Papa sorted things out, Papa had agreed

that Mama, Tina, and Daria could care for Kathleen at home. Daria had never realized how much work it took to feed and clean a growing baby.

Then the teacher had sent home a note saying that David and Daria were not keeping up with their work. Mama had spoken to them quite sternly at suppertime.

"You must do your schoolwork," she had said, "or you must face the consequences."

"What consequences?" David asked. He always managed to score well on the tests. He thought the everyday work was not important.

"You have been spending too much time playing baseball," his mother answered. "If the teacher tells me you have not improved within two weeks, you will not play baseball."

"You can't do that!" David protested. "It's my team."

"Papa says exercise is good for us," Daria added, quoting her father, the doctor, who was once again working late with patients. "Baseball is exercise."

"Learning is good for you as well," Mama said. She stirred the pot of stew one last time before ladling half of it into another pan. "After we eat, I'm going to take some supper over to the Thorntons. Mrs. Thornton had her baby today, so we have to help look after the family for a few days. When I get back, I want to find both of you in your rooms studying."

"Aw, Mama, reading is boring."

"David is further behind than I am," Daria said. "He should have to study more than I do."

"You're just as far behind as I am," David protested.

"No, I'm not."

"Yes, you are."

"No, I'm not."

"Yes, you are."

They glared at each other, brown eyes to brown eyes.

"Children, children," Mama said, "must you quarrel constantly?" She began wrapping some bread to go with the stew.

Daria and David continued glaring.

"No, I'm not," Daria whispered.

"Yes, you are!" David hissed.

"Children, children!"

"What's going on in here?" Papa appeared in the doorway, home earlier than expected from his medical clinic. With one eyebrow raised, he looked at his youngest children.

"The twins have a dispute, as usual," Mama answered.

"I don't like the tone I hear in their voices."

"I'm glad you're home early," Mama said, no longer interested in the twins' argument. "We must eat quickly so I can take the Thorntons some supper. And the twins must attend to their schoolwork tonight. Tina will take care of Kathleen."

That is how Daria ended up in her room for the entire evening. But she could not concentrate on what she was supposed to be reading. She kept thinking about TJ and David. Her brother's disputes with TJ were far worse than his quarrels with Daria.

TJ had not quit the baseball team, as he had threatened. Somehow DJ had managed to get his brother to calm down. Even Daria had talked to TJ to try to help him understand what David was like. David did not care about anything else as much as he cared about baseball. To have a real team to play on was a dream come true.

The team had played several more games, and they had won every game after losing the first one. So neither TJ nor David could claim victory about whether fielding was more important or batting was more important. As long as the team was winning, it seemed to Daria, they should stop arguing.

But the two boys kept fighting. At some practices they barely spoke to each other, and the rest of the team could feel the frustration and anger growing between them.

"Who is in charge around here?" Jake had asked one day. "David asked me to play. He said it was his team. But TJ keeps telling me how to play."

"David is just as bad," Peter countered. "He won't let me try to hurl."

When Daria overheard her teammates muttering about David and TJ, she just walked away.

Daria checked to see how many pages were left in the chapter. Too many, she quickly decided. She wondered when Tina would come upstairs to the room they shared. Tina had spent the evening at a meeting at church, but Daria was sure she had heard her return a few minutes ago.

She swung her feet over the side of the bed. Maybe a snack would help. In her stocking feet, Daria padded down the hall, down the stairs, across the sitting room, and toward the kitchen. She had her hand on the door, ready to push it open, when she heard voices.

"Are you certain of the schedule?" Tina asked.

"As certain as I can be," seventeen-year-old Charles answered. "The station master says the schedule may change at the last minute."

What was Charles talking about? Daria wondered. The schedule for trains coming in and out of Cincinnati hardly ever changed. Sometimes trains were late, though. That must be what he meant.

"How many passengers will get off at our stop?" Tina asked.

"At least seven, maybe a few more."

"Seven? All at once?"

Tina sounded alarmed, which Daria thought strange. Seven people getting off the train in Cincinnati was nothing to be concerned about.

"Are the conductors ready?" Tina asked, her voice sounding tense.

"I think so. One of the conductors is new. He's a little nervous."

Charles knew everyone who worked at the Cincinnati railroad station, Daria reminded herself. He had been obsessed with trains since he was a little boy, and now he worked there.

Daria really wanted a snack. She pushed open the kitchen door.

"Hi."

"Hello, Daria," Tina said. She looked surprised. "I thought you would be asleep by now."

"I was studying."

Charles chuckled. "You better have been studying. I heard what Mama said to you."

Daria scowled. "School is dumb."

"That's what I used to think," Charles said. "But school makes you smart—smart enough to do the things you really want to do."

Daria crossed to the ice box, a squarish cabinet with a block of ice in the bottom of it to help keep food cold. She started moving things around, searching. "I don't want to talk about school. I just want something to eat."

"If you're looking for the chocolate cake, Charles ate it," Tina said, glancing down at Kathleen, who was sleeping in a cradle at Tina's feet.

Daria pressed her lips together and darted a glance at her brother. "I should have known. You get the good stuff, and I'm stuck with a sandwich."

From the ice box, Daria pulled out a slice of ham and a jar of milk. She moved to the sideboard to find the bread and butter.

"I heard you two talking," she said, as she spread butter on the bread.

"Oh?" Tina's voice had a strange catch to it. "Just now?"

"Yes. About trains and stuff. Conductors, passengers."

"Oh."

"Charles talks about trains all the time," Daria said. She slapped the ham between the bread slices. "But I didn't know you were interested in the railroad."

"The railroad?" Tina's voice was faint, more high pitched than usual.

"What's wrong with you?" Daria asked.

"Nothing's wrong with her," Charles said. "She's fine. Let's talk about you."

"Nothing to talk about." She bit into her sandwich, then set it down on a plate.

"How's the baseball team doing?"

"We usually win." She took a sip of milk.

"I've been meaning to come and watch you play some

82

afternoon," Tina said. "I hear that you are quite a good player."

Daria looked at Tina, surprised. "Who said that?"

"David, of course."

"David said I was good? He never says that to me. He acts like he doesn't even want me on the team."

"I think he's proud of you," Charles said.

Daria shrugged her shoulders and took another bite.

"Charles," she said, "how many people get off the train every day in Cincinnati?"

Charles answered smoothly. "That's hard to say. It depends on where the train is coming from. And a lot of the trains that come through are freight trains."

"But how many people get off here?"

Charles shrugged his shoulders. "I never counted."

"About seven?" Daria asked. "Is that a lot?"

"Seven is not very many, no. I would guess dozens or hundreds."

"Oh." Daria chomped on her sandwich as she looked from Charles to Tina.

Tina stood up. "That sandwich looks good, Daria. Perhaps I'll have one, too, before I go to bed."

Daria had left everything out, so Tina busied herself fixing another sandwich.

"So did you finish studying?" Charles asked.

Daria groaned. "No. I couldn't concentrate. That's why I came down. But I suppose I'd better get back up there. I can finish this upstairs." She finished off her milk and picked up her plate with the rest of her sandwich.

"I'll be up in a few minutes," Tina said, smiling.

Daria nodded. "Good night, Charles."

She left the room. But she stopped just outside the door. Mama always said not to eavesdrop on someone else's conversation, but somehow Daria could not help herself.

"She heard us, Charles. We have to be more careful." Tina's voice was hardly more than a whisper.

"She doesn't know what's going on. I'm not worried," Charles answered. "Besides, she's the same age I was when I discovered you were involved with the Underground Railroad."

"I was not 'involved' in the Underground Railroad. I distracted one slave catcher who might have been looking for someone I knew."

Charles chuckled. "You've come a long way from that, Tina. You should be proud of yourself."

"Nevertheless, I do not want to endanger Daria. After all, she is friends with the Baxter boys. If Daria found out about Mariah, it could be dangerous for her, as well as Mariah."

Mariah? Daria wondered. The Underground Railroad? What exactly was Tina involved in, and what did it have to do with Mariah?

She held her breath and turned her ear to the door again. Tina and Charles kept their voices low. She could hardly hear them.

"Mariah is arranging passage," Tina said. "She's fond of the Baxter twins. She has taken care of them since they were babies. But she wants her own babies, and she wants them to be free. She wants to go to Canada."

Mariah? Going to Canada? How would Mariah get to Canada?

"I was hoping she would decide to go," Charles said.

Daria could hear the excitement even in her brother's low tones.

"Still, I don't want to put Daria—or David—in any danger."

Daria started to back up slowly. What kind of danger might she be in? She took a few more steps backward. The conversation in the kitchen was confusing, but it was captivating, too. She could not decide whether to stay or leave.

Daria backed into a chair and sent it tumbling on its side against the wooden floor. With her heart pounding, she scrambled to set it upright.

"Daria? Is that you?" Tina called.

Daria did not answer. She clutched her sandwich as she ran up the stairs to the safety of her room. There, she left her uneaten sandwich on the nightstand. Quickly she turned off the lights and climbed under her quilt. When Tina came to bed, Daria wanted to be found sleeping innocently.

But she could not sleep. Even with her eyes squeezed shut, she kept hearing the conversation between Charles and Tina over and over again in her mind. They were involved in the Underground Railroad. They were helping slaves escape. And they were going to help Mariah get away.

CHAPTER 10
Spying

"I won't be late, Mama," Tina said. She fastened her satin bonnet securely under her chin. "I should be home in time for lunch."

Mama looked up from the quilting hoop she held in her lap. "Take your time, Tina. It's Saturday. There's no rush. If you don't make it home, I'll keep some food warm."

"There's no need to bother, Mama."

"Are you sure you don't want to take the carriage?"

Tina shook her head. "It's a beautiful morning. I would much prefer to walk."

Daria perched on the stairs, the third step up from the bottom, and watched Tina fasten her red cloak around her shoulders. The sisters had not spoken to each other since the conversation in the kitchen the night before.

"Where are you going?" Daria asked. She did not think that was a nosy question.

Tina looked at Daria and said simply, "I have to meet someone."

"About what?"

"About some plans we need to make."

"Plans for what?" Now she was getting nosy.

"Daria, I don't have time to stand here and answer your questions right now. Aren't you supposed to be at baseball practice? David left a long time ago."

"Practice is not for an hour. He always goes early."

"And I don't want to be late." Tina smoothed the front of her cloak and glanced in the mirror next to the door. "I'll see you for lunch." She was out the door before Daria could say anything else.

Daria sat with her knees up and her elbows on her knees.

"Sit like a lady, Daria," her mother said.

Daria stuck her legs out in front of her roughly.

"Did Tina tell you who she was going to meet?" she asked her mother.

Mama pulled a careful stitch through the fabric. "Tina is a grown woman," she said. "She does not have to tell me about everything she does."

"I know! She's going to meet Enoch Stevenson," Daria said suddenly. "He's been courting her since Christmas. Maybe they are planning a wedding."

"Whatever it is, it's none of our business," her mother said.

Daria stood up and looked out the front door. She could still see Tina walking down the block.

"Mama, I'm going outside for a while," Daria said. She snatched her green wool coat off a hook next to the door.

"Come home in time for lunch," Mama said absently.

Daria slipped out the front door and walked casually in the direction Tina had gone. She had hardly slept a moment all night, after overhearing the conversation between her brother and her sister. Tina had not come upstairs to their room for a long time. Daria had pretended to be asleep, but she had heard every rustle of Tina's clothing, every creak of the wooden floor when Tina came to bed.

Enoch Stevenson came courting often at the Fisk house. Occasionally, he took Tina to a concert or to dinner with friends. But Daria did not really think her older sister was leaving the house to go meet Enoch and certainly not to plan a secret wedding. No, Tina's outing had something to do with what Daria had overheard the night before. Daria was sure of it.

Daria kept her distance about two blocks behind Tina. The bright red cloak Tina wore made it easy to follow her. Early on a Saturday morning not many people were out in the streets. Daria would have liked a crowd to hide in. Instead, she forced herself to slow down her steps and keep an even distance behind her sister. Tina never looked back. Daria was sure she did not know she was being followed.

Tina walked briskly toward their church. For a moment, Daria thought perhaps her sister was going into the gray stone building. A Saturday morning committee meeting would not be unusual. Tina was still trying to convince some of the ladies on the social concerns committee to visit the orphanage with her. But she did not go into the church. She walked right past it, hardly giving it a glance.

A few blocks farther on, they approached the street where their father had his medical clinic. Sometimes Tina went there to talk to their cousin, Meg, who worked as a nurse. But Tina did not turn into the clinic, either. She paused only to greet a patient coming out.

Tina walked and walked. Daria followed doggedly. She was getting tired. But Tina seemed not to mind the distance. Her pace never slowed, even when she walked uphill.

Suddenly Daria remembered her baseball practice! She had been so intent on following Tina that she had forgotten all about it. Now she was miles away from the practice field. She had no chance of getting there on time. For a moment she stopped walking and looked back in the direction she had come from. Perhaps she could think of some excuse for being late. No, David would not accept any excuses, especially not from Daria.

With a sigh, Daria decided to keep following Tina. She resumed her pursuit just as Tina disappeared around a corner. Daria scurried to catch up.

Tina followed the curve of the road as it led toward the southern outskirts of Cincinnati. Daria had hardly ever been out here before. The streets were not familiar at all. And they were more crowded than her neighborhood. Children played stickball in the streets. A man with a banjo sat on a crate turned upside down, strumming and humming. As she passed a blacksmith's shop, Daria scrunched up her nose at the odor. Horses lined up outside the shop, awaiting their new shoes.

Tina slowed down. She was not sure of her way around, either, and she seemed to be searching for something. Her brow furrowed in confusion, she stopped and looked around. Daria's heart leaped as she saw her sister's head turn and look in her direction. She tucked herself into the nearest doorway and held her breath. Tina turned around and continued on.

Daria's heart pumped harder. She did not want Tina to see her. But she certainly did not want to lose sight of the red cloak now. She was a long way from home. The thought of finding her way home on her own frightened her. Is this where the orphanage was? Daria wondered. Was that why Tina had come down here? Or did it have to do with stations and passengers and conductors?

Tina finally stopped. Daria stopped two blocks behind her. Her eyes darted around as she tried to figure out where she was. Every couple of seconds she glanced at Tina once again.

Tina spoke to a woman in a shop doorway and then stepped aside. She, too, seemed to be looking around, Daria thought. The shopkeeper disappeared inside. Tina leaned against the wall and watched the neighborhood. Daria hugged the brick wall again.

In a moment the shopkeeper was back with a companion. A slim dark figure in a yellow dress emerged from the dimly lit shop.

"Mariah!" Daria whispered. She was right. Tina's strange, long walk did have something to do with last night's talk.

Tina talked calmly and quietly with Mariah. Mariah did not say very much. She nodded her head a lot and glanced around nervously. Her fingers played with the edge of the bread basket she carried over one arm. That was the Baxter's bread basket. Daria had seen it before.

What was Mariah doing here? Daria wondered. This was a long way from where the Baxters lived, and many shops were closer to their neighborhood.

Tina and Mariah continued talking. Tina reached out and squeezed Mariah's shoulder. When Mariah looked at Tina, tears glimmered in her eyes.

"You'll have to move," a gruff voice said to Daria. "I need to go through there."

Daria spun around and found herself face to face with a tall, scowling man. He carried a crate loaded with vegetables.

"Move!" he said.

Daria lunged to one side. But she moved too quickly. Her foot hit a rock and she lost her balance. Tumbling to the sidewalk, she saw she was headed for the tall man's black boots. The next moment, he crashed to the sidewalk next to her. His vegetables splattered the ground.

Daria scrambled to her feet. "I'm so sorry! So sorry." She scooped up what was left of a squash and reached for some green beans.

"I only asked you to get out of the way so I could get into my shop," the man said loudly. "Now you've ruined a whole basketful of vegetables."

"I. . .I didn't mean to. I fell."

"Clumsy child!"

Daria was still scooping up the damaged vegetables. Some of them were bruised, some of them were ruined.

The man pushed her roughly away. "Just go away," he said. "Leave before you cause more trouble."

Swallowing hard, Daria nodded and moved away quickly. She looked around. Two other shopkeepers had seen the collision and were snickering in amusement. But other people in the street were minding their own business.

Fortunately, Tina was still concentrating on her conversation with Mariah. Daria breathed a sigh of relief as she once again leaned against a wall—this time staying clear of any doorways.

A moment later, Tina gave Mariah a quick hug and they separated. Tina turned around and began walking toward Daria. With her heart in her throat, Daria ducked into the shop. She had to get home without being discovered, but she needed to follow Tina's red cloak to get home safely. She would just wait for Tina to pass the shop on her way home and then follow again.

Glancing at the shop door every few seconds, Daria picked up a tea cup to admire. The green floral pattern around the rim reminded her of the quilt on her bed.

When someone tapped her on the shoulder, she nearly dropped the tea cup. Turning around, she could not even raise her head. As soon as she saw the red cloak, she knew she was in trouble.

"Shopping for vegetables?" Tina asked, amused.

Daria looked up at her sister with wide eyes. "You saw what happened?"

"Everyone on the block saw what happened," Tina said. "What I want to know is what you are doing down here in the first place."

Daria looked down at her shoes. "I'm sorry. I was just curious about where you were going."

"So you followed me."

Daria nodded.

Tina sighed. "Daria Fisk, ever since you were a baby, you've had a mind of your own. I can be sure that you will always do exactly as you please."

"I'm sorry."

"Mama would not be happy to know you came down here alone."

Daria had no response. What Tina said was true.

"At least I'll make sure you get home safely."

"Are you helping Mariah get to Canada?" Daria blurted out.

Tina was silent for a moment as they walked. "You heard Charles and me talking last night, didn't you?"

"I'm sorry about that, too," Daria muttered. "I couldn't help it."

Tina sighed again and spoke in a low voice. "Keep walking," she said. "Yes, I am helping Mariah. She wants to be free."

"But Mariah can go anywhere she wants to," Daria said. "She's not like the slaves in the South. She goes shopping, and she has her own room at the Baxter's house. Even I don't have my own room. I have to share with you."

"But she's not free," Tina said. "The Baxters could sell her at a slave market any time they wanted to."

"Mrs. Baxter would never do that! She says she can't live without Mariah."

"Well, Mariah wants to live without Mrs. Baxter. She wants her own house, and her own family. And I think she should have it."

"You agree with Papa, don't you?" Daria asked. "You think that the Southern states should stop having slaves."

"Yes, I do," Tina said confidently. "I think slavery is morally wrong."

"Were you really my age when you started working in the Underground Railroad?"

"I was a little older. Charles was your age." Tina chuckled and kept walking. "You almost kept me from it."

"What do you mean?"

"You were four, and you wandered off to find the candy shop. I was looking everywhere for you and almost lost sight of the slave catcher. Thank goodness Charles found you and took you home so I could concentrate on what I needed to do."

"That's when you helped the Underground Railroad?"

Tina nodded. "I guess you could say that. I just got in somebody's way long enough for someone else to get away."

"Were you afraid?"

"Yes. But it was the right thing to do. I couldn't just walk away and let something awful happen."

"DJ says that South Carolina does not like people in the north telling them what to do."

Tina nodded. "Yes, that's the other problem. Many of the states want to decide for themselves whether or not to have slaves. They don't want to be told what to do."

"Just like David."

Tina looked puzzled. "David?"

"He doesn't want anyone telling him what to do with the baseball team," Daria explained. She groaned. "And he's going to be really, really mad at me for missing practice."

CHAPTER 11

Who's in Charge?

"Are you sure you want to come?" Daria asked. She could not believe her sister was truly interested in coming to watch a baseball practice with a bunch of ten-year-olds. Weeks had passed since Tina had said she wanted to see the team. Suddenly that morning she had decided this was the day.

"Absolutely certain," Tina responded. "I used to do things with the two of you all the time when you were younger. I don't know why that changed. Besides, I have some good news for you."

They were walking briskly toward the schoolyard. Waiting for Tina had made Daria late for practice.

"What news?" Daria asked.

"Meg stopped by this morning. She and Papa thought they recognized Kathleen from a case they were treating down at the clinic. They have determined that young Mrs. O'Grady is indeed Kathleen's mother. She was heartbroken over giving Kathleen up, but she didn't see how she could give Kathleen the care she needed when there literally was no food in the house. Pride kept her from asking for help."

"So what happens now?" Daria asked.

"Meg's going to ask Aunt Dot and Uncle Tim if they can take Mrs. O'Grady on as live-in help with her baby. That way Kathleen could be with her mama, and Mrs. O'Grady would have a good place to live and work."

Daria squealed in excitement. "They must say yes," she said. "They must!"

"We'll see," Tina replied. "In the meantime we should continue to pray for little Kathleen and her mama. Now, explain to me a little bit about your baseball."

"It's just a practice," Daria said. "It's not even a game."

"Perhaps I'll come to a game, too. I understand you win all your games."

Daria smiled. "Except the first one. But we're going to play that team again, and this time we'll win!"

"That's the spirit."

"We have to win," Daria muttered as she kicked a loose rock. "If we lose, David will blame it all on me."

"How could he possibly do that? You're just one person on the team."

"He was really mad when I missed the practice the other day."

"It was just one practice."

"David doesn't see it that way."

"He does seem to be a bit of a grouch lately."

They came to the edge of the playing field. Tina stopped abruptly and scanned the field.

"Something's wrong," she said. "I'm not an expert on

baseball like you and David, but this is not right. Look, that boy over there is just standing there, doing nothing. And he looks very unhappy."

"That's TJ," Daria said flatly. "If you think David's been grouchy, wait until you talk to TJ."

"TJ? Isn't he one of the Baxter twins you talk about all the time?"

Daria nodded and pointed toward DJ out in the field. "There's his brother."

"Yes, I remember meeting them at the picnic in August. Mariah has talked about them. But what's the matter with TJ?" Tina asked. "Why isn't he playing with the others?"

Daria shrugged. "He wants to do things one way, and David has other ideas."

They looked over toward David, who was hitting fly balls. The rest of the team was scattered across the field, running after the balls and throwing them back in toward David.

"David and TJ have been fighting," Daria explained. "Almost every time we have a practice, they argue. They both want to have the best team around, but they have different ideas about what we should be doing when we practice. Most of the boys have been listening more to David. That just makes TJ madder."

"What about DJ?" asked Tina. "How does he feel?"

"He just wants to play baseball."

Tina pressed her lips together. "This certainly cannot continue. It's no way for a team to operate. You must do something, Daria."

"Me! What can I do? It's David and TJ who are always fighting."

Tina nudged Daria's elbow. "Somebody has to be reasonable. I remember David saying how much he liked the Baxter boys. Go talk to TJ. See if you can get him to join the others."

"Aw, Tina," Daria protested.

"Go on."

Reluctantly, Tina shuffled toward TJ. Occasionally he tossed a ball a few inches in the air and caught it. But most of the time, he just stood there glowering at the rest of the team. If he saw Daria approach, he did not show it.

"Hi, TJ," Daria said. She tried to make her voice sound as friendly as possible.

He did not respond.

"How's the practice going so far?"

"You have eyes," he said curtly. "Use 'em." His own eyes were fixed on David. Daria could see the redness rising in his pale cheeks.

Daria took a breath and tried again. "Looks like we're working on fielding skills today. That's good."

TJ shook his head. "He's doing it all wrong. He's not hitting hard enough. Those are not like the hits in a real game."

Daria stood and watched as David tossed several balls in the air and swung at them. TJ was right. Everything David hit was easy to catch or stop. The team looked much better than they really were.

"Maybe you should throw to him," Daria suggested. "Then he'd have to hit like it was a real game."

TJ did not say anything. He did not change his expression.

Daria tried to think of something else to say, but she

could not. Finally, she just left and returned to Tina.

"I told you it wouldn't do any good," Daria whined. "He won't even talk to me."

"At least you tried," Tina said. "Now how about talking to David?"

"That won't do any good, either," Daria said.

"When you were little, you could get David to do whatever you wanted," Tina said.

"Not anymore," Daria said. "He's got a mind of his own now. He doesn't really care what I think."

"You have to try," Tina said gently.

Daria sighed and then nodded. With all the other boys out in the field to catch the balls David hit, she could talk to him without anyone overhearing. She walked over to where he was swinging the bat over and over.

"I need to talk to you, David," she said.

David tossed a ball in the air and swung at it. It lobbed toward center field.

"You're late," he said.

"I know. I'm sorry." She picked up a ball and handed it to him. He threw it in the air and swung at it.

"You missed the last practice," David growled, "and you came late to this one. I'm beginning to wonder if you really want to be on this team."

"Of course I do. I'm the best midfielder you've got."

"That doesn't matter if you're not here." He threw another ball up and smacked it to right field.

"David, TJ shouldn't be over there all by himself. He's the best hurler you've ever seen. We're lucky to have him on the team."

"He doesn't have to be by himself. He can come and

join the practice anytime he wants to."

"You should go talk to him."

David grunted as he swung hard at another ball. Daria took a step away from the bat.

"He wanted us to practice fielding," David said, "so we're practicing fielding. What more does he want?"

"David, talk to him. Listen to him."

David shook his head. "If he wants to talk to me, he knows where I am."

He hit another ball.

"Tina's here," Daria said.

David glanced over his shoulder and saw his older sister. "Why?" he asked.

"She just wanted to watch."

"Tina doesn't like baseball."

Daria rolled her eyes. "Maybe not, but she came to watch us."

"She's not going to make us stop, is she?"

"Of course not."

A ball came rolling across the grass toward David's feet. "Nice throw!" he called out to Lars.

"Are you here to practice or not?" David asked as he hit another ball.

"Yes, of course."

"Then get out in the field."

Daria turned toward Tina and shrugged. She had done what Tina had asked. She had tried to talk to David. A glance in TJ's direction told her he had not moved.

In no particular hurry, Daria scuffed her way out to left field. She found a clear spot and got ready to start fielding balls.

David swung and hit a ball that barely made it out of the infield. Peter scooped it up and lobbed it back to David. Conrad caught the next one easily. Then Lars retrieved a ground ball that had sputtered to a stop in front of him.

Daria held up her hand to block the sun in her eyes. If TJ were not off to the side scowling, it would look like a good practice. The team seemed to be having fun. Maybe David and TJ were taking the baseball team too seriously. Maybe the other boys did not care if they won every single game or not.

"He's making it too easy," said a voice behind her.

Daria turned to see DJ walking toward her. "That's what TJ said," she responded. "He's not hitting them hard enough."

"He keeps hitting them in the same spots, too. Nothing has come my way the whole time I've been out here."

"DJ, are you having fun?"

He looked at her, surprised by the question. "What do you mean?"

"Is the team any fun? TJ won't even practice, and David is grouchy all the time. I'm not sure this is fun anymore."

DJ nodded. "I know what you mean. I like winning. We have a really good team. Almost everybody is good at something—even you!" He grinned at her.

She stuck her tongue out at him. "If everybody is so good, and the team is winning, why are we all so unhappy?"

As they talked, they drifted toward the third base side of the field.

DJ rubbed his toe in the dirt. "Sometimes I feel like

wringing TJ's neck. He's so stubborn!"

"I know what you mean," Daria said. "I can hardly talk to David anymore."

"But TJ is my brother—my twin. And I don't like to be fighting with him all the time."

"Me, neither," Daria agreed. "TJ is right some of the time. David just won't listen."

"And sometimes David is right," DJ said. "But if I point that out to TJ, he just gets mad at me."

"Sometimes I feel like pretending I don't know David, even if he is my twin brother."

"Hey!"

They turned to see that it was David bellowing at them.

"What are you two doing out there? Get back on the field!"

Daria rolled her head to one side and sighed. "Here we go again."

"We are here to practice, after all," DJ said. "We'd better do what he wants."

They started moving toward the playing area once again.

"What are you, a couple of wimps?" This time it was TJ yelling at them. "Do you do everything he tells you to do? Can't you think for yourselves?"

David threw down his bat and charged at TJ.

"You keep out of this," he screamed. "If you don't want to practice, fine. But you can't interfere with what the rest of us want to do."

TJ threw his ball to the ground. "Did you even ask the rest of them what they want to do? I doubt it. You always do exactly what you want to do, no matter what anyone else says."

By now David and TJ were standing only a few inches apart. The other players were scrambling in from the outfield to see what would happen next.

"Speak up," TJ challenged them. "Say what you want to do. Take a vote. You don't have to let David be a Northern dictator."

"That's better than being a spineless Southerner, who doesn't even have the courage to do the right thing."

"Y'all don't think about how your decisions affect anyone else. You won't let Peter be a hurler when I know he'd be a good one."

"I do what I think is good for the team," David said in his own defense. "Do you think you're doing the team any good standing over there all by yourself?"

"You're hitting balls that a baby slave could catch." TJ reached out and nudged David's shoulder with one hand.

David stumbled backward a step or two and quickly recovered. "Keep your hands off of me, I'm warning you!"

"Warning me? You couldn't do anything to hurt me."

"Just watch me!"

"Go ahead! I dare you! Take a punch." TJ spread his feet apart and squared off against David. His fists curled in front of his chest. His face was three shades redder than Daria had ever seen it.

Daria looked over at Tina and raised her hands. What was she supposed to do next? Tina was on her way over.

"What's the matter?" TJ taunted. "I said go ahead and hit me. Why don't you do it? Are you chicken?"

"I'm not afraid of you," David said.

"Do something," Daria pleaded, when Tina arrived. "They're going to hurt each other."

"David Fisk, you stop this nonsense," Tina said loudly.

David glanced over at her, but he quickly turned his attention back to TJ.

"Talking to them won't work," Daria said aloud. She grabbed DJ's elbow with one hand and Conrad's arm with the other. "Come on. We came here to practice. So let's practice. We don't need either of them."

Boldly, she led the way back to the outfield, dragging DJ and Conrad with her. Out of the side of her eye, she could see that Peter, Lars, Jimmy, and Tad were coming along as well.

"I think David should let TJ have it," Lars said.

"TJ's bigger," Conrad argued. "If he really wanted to, he could beat David up with no trouble at all."

"Naw, I don't think so. David moves so fast TJ could never get near him."

Daria turned and stared at the boys behind her. "You act like you want them to fight."

Conrad shrugged. "Maybe they would get it out of their systems. What would it hurt?"

Daria could not believe her ears. "What does fighting have to do with playing on a baseball team?" she demanded. "Don't any of you want to play baseball?"

She threw the ball in her hand down as hard and furiously as she could. Then she stomped off. Daria was going home.

CHAPTER 12

A New President

"Are you almost ready?" Tina asked Daria the next day.

"Just about." Daria reached for her coat. It was the day of the social concerns committee meeting at the church. "It certainly is quiet without Kathleen here." Meg's mama was caring for Kathleen that day. Daria glanced around the foyer. "Where's Mama?"

"She's gone ahead," Tina answered. "She and Meg will meet us there."

"Did they take the carriage?"

Tina smiled. "No, they left the carriage for us."

Daria grinned. "Mama thinks I'm lazy, but I like to take the carriage."

"It is a bit nippy outside these days."

Daria tightened her coat around her neck against the brisk, late October air. "I'm ready."

They went outside. Daria patted the gray mare before climbing up into the carriage.

"Can I drive?" she asked.

"Does Mama let you drive?" Tina asked.

"Well, not exactly," Daria said. "But she keeps saying that soon I'll be old enough."

"Scoot over here," Tina said, patting the empty spot beside her. "We'll drive together. Let's just say it's your first lesson."

Daria gladly slid closer to her sister and reached out to grip the reins. The mare began her trot.

"You're not missing a practice to come to this meeting, are you?" Tina asked.

Daria shook her reddish curls. "No. Not today. And even if there were a practice, I think I'd skip it."

"Really?" Tina said, surprised. "I thought you loved playing."

"I do—when we get to play. I'm just tired of David and TJ fighting all the time."

Tina nodded. "That was quite a display yesterday. They hardly even noticed when you left. But then everyone else left, too, and it was just the two of them standing there arguing."

"Did you stay to watch?"

Tina nodded. "I was hoping to be able to talk to David. He was such a sweet child when he was small. I can hardly believe that was the same boy."

"It's David, all right. I've always known he could be a terror."

Tina chuckled. "I suppose twins know these things before anyone else."

"That's right." Daria jiggled the reins authoritatively. "Did you get David to listen to you?"

Tina shook her head. "No."

"It's hopeless," Daria moaned.

"Don't give up!" Tina said. "There has to be a solution that makes everyone happy."

"I don't know what to say to either of them," Daria said. "Sometimes I think I would be better off living with the orphans."

"At least you're doing something to help the orphans."

"Yes, but what can I do once Kathleen leaves? I just know Aunt Dot and Uncle Tim will give her mother a job."

"I'm certain you will want to donate one or two of your dresses to the clothing drive."

Daria grinned. "Will you take my pinafore?"

"Gladly, ruffles and all." Tina's expression got serious again. "And don't give up on David."

Daria shrugged. "At least there is only one more game. Then it will be all over."

"But what about next year?" Tina asked. "Won't the team get together again in the spring?"

"I can't even think about the spring," Daria said. "I just want to get through the last game."

Tina pulled up at the church and let Daria hitch the horse. They walked into the meeting room, which was already filled with the usual group of women. Once again refreshments were laid out on a lace-covered table, and once again Mrs. Baxter had joined the group.

Daria hurried over to Mama, and the ladies quickly found their seats.

"Good afternoon, ladies," Tina began, taking a seat next to Daria. "I see many of you have brought clothing for the orphans today. This will be a fine start to our work."

The ladies murmured in agreement.

"During the past month," Tina continued, "have any of you had some ideas of other things we could do to help?"

After a moment of silence, Meg said, "I was thinking that perhaps we could spend a few minutes each day sewing for the little ones. We could even sew for them during our meetings or perhaps have quilting parties. I was noticing that their bed linens were in short supply."

"What a fine idea," Mrs. Wyeth said. "I know I said I was already sewing for the Underground Railroad, but I imagine I can find a few minutes each day to work on something for the children."

At the mention of the Underground Railroad, Daria felt her stomach tighten. At the last meeting, no one had actually spoken the words aloud. Her eyes darted to Mrs. Baxter, who was getting red in the face, just as TJ did when he was mad.

"I cannot believe," Mrs. Baxter said, "that you can sit here in a church, the house of God, and openly admit that you have been aiding the Underground Railroad. You must know that such behavior is against the law."

"It may be against the law of the South," Mrs. Wyeth retorted, "but it is not against God's law."

"We established during our last meeting that God is not

a Baptist or a Methodist. Perhaps you now believe him to be a Northerner?"

"I never said that," Mrs. Wyeth said calmly. "I'm simply sewing clothes for people less fortunate than I."

"I assure you that we in the South are true Christians," Mrs. Baxter said, her voice rising. "We are only doing what God blessed us to do when He created the races."

Daria gripped her hands together in her lap and leaned over toward Tina. "Now I know where TJ gets his attitude from," she whispered.

Tina did not respond. The color had drained from her face.

Daria looked back at the group. No one answered Mrs. Baxter.

"No one wants a war," Mrs. Baxter asserted. "But we will not have the wishes of the North imposed upon the South."

"Perhaps we should go back to discussing the orphans," Meg said, standing up abruptly. "At least we can all agree that the orphans need our help."

Many of the women shifted in their seats and looked away from Deborah Baxter. Meg launched into a discussion of the types of clothes they could sew and the quilt patterns they could use.

Daria looked again at her sister. "Tina," she whispered, "do you think there is going to be a war?"

Tina's green eyes met Daria's brown ones. "I'm afraid it's already begun."

Early November brought a winter chill that settled heavily over Cincinnati. Daria was glad that Uncle Tim and Aunt

Dot had agreed to hire Mrs. O'Grady. Although she missed Kathleen and the house was quieter without the baby, Daria was thankful Mrs. O'Grady didn't have to deal with the cold in the miserable shack she'd been living in. She would never forget the joy on Mrs. O'Grady's face when Daria had placed little Kathleen in her arms.

After weeks of debate, early November also brought the presidential election. With telegraphs, the November 6 election results could be tallied much more quickly than in the old days. By the next morning the results were clear. Abraham Lincoln had been elected president. He had won against three other candidates, and most of David and Daria's friends were excited about the results.

"Down with Southern slavery!" one boy yelled before school that morning just after the news had broken.

"Three cheers for Lincoln!" yelled another student.

"That'll teach those dirty Southerners a thing or two!"

Someone started singing "America," and soon everybody was joining in, marching around the playground. That is, *almost* everybody. Daria noticed that TJ and DJ were standing off to the side being very quiet, and TJ looked angrier than she had ever seen him. She shivered as the bell rang, signaling the beginning of school.

Winter was on the way, and that meant the end of the baseball season. Even David finally admitted that it was getting too cold to play baseball. The coats Mama had the twins wear made it hard to move around. Standing in the outfield at practice, Daria spent most of her time rubbing her hands together, trying to keep her fingers from turning red. When she exhaled, her warm breath hung in the air in front of her before dissolving into the cold.

But the team had one more game to play. As soon as they had lost the first game they played, David decided that they would play that team again—and win. They had easily won every other game they played—mostly because of TJ's great pitching. So David fixed his sights on a rematch. And now the day had come.

Daria was pretty sure they were ready to win this game—and she wanted to win as much as David did. But she did wish that the sun would shine more brightly. It was going to be a cold afternoon.

As usual, she was late getting to the playing field. By the time she got there, all the other players on the team were gathered, and most of the players from the other team.

Daria stopped in her tracks. She groaned at what she saw in front of her. The team was gathered in a huddle, but not for a pep talk or instructions from David. They were watching TJ and David barely keep from tearing each other apart. David's brown eyes bulged, and TJ's gray eyes had more fire in them than Daria had ever seen before.

She debated about how badly she wanted to play in this last game. She could just turn around and go home and pretend she had not seen the two boys locked in a glare of hostility.

"Daria!" someone called.

Conrad had seen her. Daria groaned again. He came running toward her.

"You have to do something," Conrad said. "They're doing it again, and it's getting really ugly."

"It was ugly the last time," Daria said.

"This is worse."

"I don't care about this stupid baseball game. It's too

cold out here anyway. I'm going home."

Conrad grabbed her arm. "You can't do that." He glanced over at DJ standing to one side. "You and DJ are twins to David and TJ. You have to make them stop so we can play. The other team is watching!"

Daria looked at TJ and David. Their voices had risen to screams that everyone on the field could hear.

"You have to hurl, TJ," David insisted. "This is the final game. This is the only team we haven't beaten. You have to hurl!"

"I don't have to do anything I don't want to do," TJ hissed. "You can't make me, so don't even try."

"Are you going to stand there and tell me that you don't want to beat the socks off this team?"

TJ glared at David. "I want to beat them," TJ said. "That's why I think we need to play the game my way."

"You always want your own way," David growled. "You're a true Southerner all right. You want to do things your way no matter how it affects anyone else."

"Don't you insult the South!"

"Why are Southerners so stubborn?"

"Why are Northerners so bossy? Y'all think you can tell us what to do—how to hurl, whether we can have slaves. It's none of your business what we do in the South. Keep your nose out of it."

"This team is my business," David said. "And you're a member of the team."

"I don't have to be a member of this team. I could start my own team. At least half the players would come with me. We don't need you to have a good team."

Daria looked at DJ. He looked just as frustrated as she

felt. Their eyes met, and slowly she nodded her head. She put up her fingers in a count: one, two, three.

On the count of three, DJ and Daria charged at their twins and yanked them apart. David was taller than Daria. She grabbed him around the waist from behind and mustered every ounce of strength to knock him off balance. After wrestling him to the ground, she sat victoriously on his chest.

David looked at her, stunned.

"What are you doing?" he demanded.

"I'm trying to make you behave like a human being," Daria said. She pushed on his shoulders with the heels of her hands.

"Ow! Stop that!"

"Are you ready to listen to me?"

"Are you going to get off of me?"

"No. Not until you listen."

"All right. Talk."

"TJ Baxter is the best hurler you have ever seen," Daria said. "He's even better than you. Maybe that's what bothers you so much. He's right. He could go play on another team, and they would beat the daylights out of us. You need him, David. You need TJ to throw for us."

"That's what I've been trying to tell him." He tried to wriggle free. Daria bounced slightly on his chest. David grunted under the fresh pressure.

"You've been trying to tell him how to pitch, how to field, how to do everything. When someone is as good at baseball as TJ is, you should be listening to him!"

"It's my team!"

"It's our team," Daria corrected. "Everybody counts.

TJ needs you just as much as you need him."

Keeping a firm grip on David's shoulders, Daria glanced over at the Baxters. DJ had his twin in a similar hold and was talking earnestly very close to his face.

"I think DJ is just about finished with TJ. I want you to get up, go over there, and shake TJ's hand."

"Are you crazy?"

"If you don't, he won't throw and we'll lose this game."

David did not answer. Conrad, Lars, Peter, and Jimmy were inching closer to hear what he would say. The other members of the team were closing in on the Baxter boys.

"The other team is warming up," Daria said. "They're concentrating on playing ball, not fighting with each other."

"Oh, all right," David said, trying once again to free himself. This time Daria let him up.

She stood up and brushed off her skirt. The back of David's coat and pants were covered with dirt. Daria would have to explain that to her mother later.

"How can you criticize me for fighting after what you just did?" David demanded.

"I waited as long as I could," Daria said. "Mama's not going to be happy when she finds out. But I had to get your attention." She pointed at TJ, who was on his feet again, too. "Now go!"

With his jaw set firmly, David shuffled over to TJ and stuck out his hand. TJ hesitated. DJ poked him in the ribs, hard. TJ's hand jerked out and shook David's for about half a second.

David turned around and shouted to the team, "Let's play ball. Take your positions. Let's win this one!"

Daria sighed heavily and started her trek out to midfield. At that moment, winning did not seem very important. When her mother found out what she had done to David, she was probably going to have to spend the rest of the week in her room.

By the middle of the third inning, the twins' team was ahead four runs to three. The game still had two more innings, and a lot could happen in two innings. Daria trotted in from midfield, wishing that she could get her hands warmed up. Just before dropping to the ground with the other players waiting their turn to bat, she spotted Tina.

"What are you doing here?" she asked.

"This was my last chance to see you in action," Tina said brightly. "Besides, I thought you might want something hot to drink." She held up a jar of hot sweet tea and a mug.

"Is there enough for everyone?" Daria asked, as she eagerly reached for the steaming mug.

"Of course." Tina produced some more cups, and they started passing around the hot liquid.

Conrad stepped up to the plate and hit a strong base hit to right field. Their half of the inning was off to a good start.

"Are TJ and David getting along?" Tina asked.

Daria shook her head and wrapped her fingers around the warm mug. "They're not fighting, but they're not getting along, either."

Peter snapped a line drive over the shortstop's head. Conrad was on his way to third.

"Tell me what happened," Tina urged.

Daria told Tina the whole story of how she and DJ had

tackled the twins and forced them to shake hands.

"I had to beat David up to keep him from beating up TJ," she said. "That doesn't make sense. And he's just as mad as he ever was."

They watched silently as Lars struck out.

In the end, they won the game seven to five. Conrad, Lars, Peter, and the others whooped and hollered their way across the field as they headed off to their homes. Even DJ's eyes glowed with pleasure. But David and TJ acted like the afternoon had been just a bad practice. They did not speak to each other. They had now beaten every other team. They were the only team in the neighborhood to do that. It was a moment of victory. But they only glared at each other, collected their equipment, and started walking in separate directions.

DJ and Daria drifted over to Tina.

"That was a spectacular last inning!" Tina said. "DJ, your home run to left field was incredible."

DJ muttered his thanks for the compliment.

"And you won," Tina continued. "You're champions now."

Daria shook her head. Her eyes followed David trailing across the field toward home. His bat thumped along behind him. "Then why doesn't it feel like we won anything?"

Chapter 13

A Broken Friendship

"You must take time to eat breakfast," Mama said to her older daughter.

"I have an early appointment at the orphanage," Tina said. She was draining the last of her cocoa from a mug. "I don't want to be late."

Daria, dressed in a light gray woolen dress, slipped into the kitchen, to join her family for breakfast. The mid-December morning was chilly. Daria had shivered as she dressed in her unheated bedroom. She knew it would be April before she would be warm in the mornings again. Her mother insisted that the family eat a hot breakfast together on cold days. Daria was glad for the warmth of the kitchen as she snuggled her way in between Tina and Charles and settled into a chair across from David.

"You have to eat," Mama repeated. She set a plate with three hotcakes smothered in butter in front of Tina.

"Your mother's right," Papa said. "I don't want you skipping meals."

Daria snickered. Even though Tina was a grown woman—was being courted and running a church com- mittee—sometimes Mama just had to be Mama. Tina was going to have to eat those hotcakes whether she wanted them or not.

Tina sighed and gave in. She picked up a fork and broke off a steaming bite.

"I'll take six, please." Daria said. Putting something warm in her stomach was appealing.

Her mother gave her a doubtful look as she poured more batter into the sizzling skillet.

"How many do you want, David?" Mama asked.

"Twelve."

If Daria had said ten, David would have said twenty.

"What is the appointment for?" Charles asked. He reached across the table for the molasses and drowned his own hotcakes in the dark liquid.

"I have some clothes to deliver," Tina explained, taking another bite. "Everything we've collected has been washed and mended. I wanted to take the first load over myself. I have to go to the church first and load the carriage."

"Did you get a lot of things?" Daria asked. Her mouth watered at the sight and smell of her sister's hotcakes.

"We got quite a bit," Tina said. "Mrs. Wyeth was especially helpful with the mending. Even Mrs. Baxter contributed a few of her boys' things."

David's ears perked up. "Mrs. Baxter? She gave away some of TJ and DJ's clothes?"

"I'm sure they were things that did not fit anymore," Tina said.

"I thought Mrs. Baxter had decided to quit your committee," Charles said.

"She has," Tina answered. "After Mr. Lincoln was elected president, she simply did not feel she could fit in with the other ladies. But she sent someone with the clothes."

"Probably Mariah," David said.

"No," Tina said quietly. "Mariah's gone."

"What do you mean, Mariah's gone?" David pressed. "Where would she go?"

Tina threw a glance at Daria. "She's just gone."

"Back to South Carolina?"

Tina was quiet. She chewed slowly and poured herself some more coffee.

"Did Mariah go to South Carolina or not?" David demanded.

"No. She had a railroad ticket north." Tina stabbed a bit of hotcake and moved it to her mouth.

Everyone was silent while David figured out what Tina was talking about—except that she was not really talking about it.

"I'm sure Mrs. Baxter misses Mariah," Mama said. "I do believe she was genuinely fond of her." She set full plates in front of Daria and David, an even six cakes each. They battled each other to reach for the molasses first. Daria won.

119

"Twins, please," Mama pleaded, "there is plenty of molasses to go around."

"I think all Southerners are a bunch of troublemakers," David declared. "The committee will be better off without Mrs. Baxter anyway." He grabbed the molasses from his twin.

"David!" Papa said harshly. "You're being disrespectful of your friends' mother."

"TJ and DJ are not my friends," David said adamantly.

"Well, they are my friends," Daria said just as adamantly. "You could be friends, too, if you really wanted to be."

"Hah! TJ has not even spoken to me at school since the last game. That was more than a month ago."

"Do you blame him?" Daria said accusingly. "You didn't exactly try to be nice to him."

David shrugged. "I know we didn't agree on everything."

"You argued about everything!"

"But that's over. The season is done. If he weren't such a Southern snob, he would talk to me."

"David, I will not warn you again," their father said. "You will not speak about other people with such a tone."

David hung his head sullenly and concentrated on his hotcakes.

Daria shoved her plate away.

"You've hardly touched your breakfast," her mother said. "Eat."

"I'm not hungry," Daria muttered.

"A moment ago you were ready to steal my food," Tina said.

"I'm just not hungry anymore."

"Whether the Southerners like it or not, times are changing." Charles stuffed another forkful in his mouth. He was not interested in Daria's change in appetite. "President Lincoln is going to change things. He wants the country unified. The question of slavery must be settled once and for all."

"I hate the thought of a war," Papa said, shaking his head sadly. "So many will die, and thousands of others will be maimed. But I'm afraid war is in the wind."

"DJ says that the Southern states just want to be able to decide for themselves," Daria said, "that it's not fair that the people in the North have their own way when the Southerners don't want the same thing."

"Of course he would say that," David said. "DJ's a nice kid, but he's a Southerner through and through."

Daria stood up abruptly and took her plate to the sink. There she dropped it harder than she should have. Behind her, Mama jumped.

"Daria, what's wrong?" Tina asked.

"Nothing." She threw her fork into the sink with equal force.

"You're acting just like you always do when you're bothered about something."

Daria did not answer.

Tina brought her plate to the sink and stood beside Daria.

After a moment, Daria spoke softly. "I don't want there to be a war."

"No one does." Tina put a gently hand on Daria's shoulder.

"Then why is there going to be one? Why is God letting the war happen?"

"We're not sure there is going to be a war. But if there is, we have to look for what God wants us to do about it."

"Like the orphans?"

"What do you mean?" Tina asked.

"No one wants children to be orphans," Daria said. "But some children are, and we have to do what we can to help. That's what you think, isn't it?"

Behind them, a chair scraped the wooden floor.

"I have to get to the clinic," Papa said. He pushed his plate aside and stood up.

"I'm late, too," Charles said.

Tina squeezed Daria's shoulder and said, "I have to get going."

Within five minutes, the kitchen was cleared out. Mama was left with the remains of her family's breakfast, while everyone else went where they were supposed to be.

Daria and David were supposed to be on their way to school. With their lunch buckets slung over their shoulders and one last reminder from their mother to button their coats, they closed the door behind them and headed up the street.

"Why do you say such mean things about TJ?" Daria asked. Now that they were alone, she could say whatever was on her mind. "He's really smart, you know. He has some great ideas."

"But he wants his ideas to be my ideas. That's the problem." David picked up a pebble and tossed it casually down the street.

"You should try to get along," Daria insisted. "You two

are a great combination if you just keep from yelling at each other all the time."

"Don't lecture me," David said sullenly. He nodded across the street. "Here come your friends now."

Daria caught DJ's eye. Sometimes it was hard to be friends with TJ when she knew how TJ felt about her own twin. But being with DJ was easy. She had long ago forgiven him for hitting her on the head with a baseball at their first meeting. She had managed to get her seat at school changed so she could sit next to DJ.

Leaving David behind, Daria crossed the street to walk with the Baxter twins.

They were walking fast. Daria broke into a slow trot to keep up.

"Why are you running?" she asked.

"We're not running," TJ answered without looking at her.

Daria looked at DJ, puzzled. DJ shrugged.

"My sister said your mother gave some clothes to the collection for the orphans. That was nice."

"She didn't ask us," TJ said, his eyes straight ahead. He walked even faster.

Daria was running and beginning to feel out of breath. Still, the boys did not slow down. TJ set the pace, and DJ kept in step. So far, DJ had not spoken.

"Did she give away anything you wanted?" Daria asked.

"Nah."

"What is wrong with you today?" Daria demanded. Her patience was exhausted.

TJ halted, spun around, and glowered at Daria. "You know what's wrong. Mariah is gone, and your sister had something to do with it."

Daria was stunned. "You don't know that for sure." Even she did not know exactly what Tina might have done to help Mariah go to Canada.

"Yes, I do. Your sister and your mother and all those other committee ladies—they're a bunch of criminals."

"Don't say that about my sister!"

"Mariah belonged to my mother. It's against the law to help slaves escape, even in the North. Your sister had no right to take her away."

"Tina didn't take Mariah away. Mariah left! She's a human being, and she has a mind of her own."

"My papa paid a good price for her. Are you going to pay him back for what he's lost?"

His gray eyes glared at her. Her hands crossed in front of her, Daria stared back.

Finally TJ spun on his heel, turned around, and resumed his half-run to school.

Daria caught DJ's arm before he could get away. She looked into his eyes, looking for the softer shade of gray she had seen so often before.

DJ shifted his eyes away from her. He did not speak. She dropped his arm and let him go.

David stood behind her. "Now do you understand why I have a problem with TJ?"

"It's stupid! The whole thing is stupid!"

DJ had refused even to look at her. Daria's eyes filled with tears that she refused to let flow.

That evening, Papa came home with more bad news. "South Carolina has voted to secede from the Union if

Mr. Lincoln is inaugurated in March," he announced.

"Oh, no!" Mama exclaimed, covering her mouth with her hand.

"What does it mean to secede?" David asked.

"It means that they don't want to be part of the United States any longer," Papa answered. "They want to be a separate country. Some of the other Southern states may decide to do the same thing."

"Why?" Daria asked. "How can a state decide not to be a state?"

"As you know, Mr. Lincoln was elected president last month," Papa explained. "The people of South Carolina are not happy about that because of his position against slavery."

"But he won the election, fair and square," David pointed out.

"That may be true," Papa said, "but that doesn't mean much to the Southern states. They do not want slavery to be abolished, and it appears they are willing to do anything to keep the government from telling them what to do—even if it means forming a new country. We'll have to wait and see if other states join South Carolina and if they actually do secede once Mr. Lincoln takes office."

"Yes," Mama said. "We'll have to wait and pray. Pray that our country can stay united."

CHAPTER 14

Breaking Away

"I thought Miss Hampton was never going to let us out today!" Conrad threw down his empty lunch bucket at the edge of the schoolyard. He hurled himself onto the spring grass and rolled over three times.

Tad followed Conrad's lead. "I'm just glad spring is here," he said. "I hate winter."

David grinned down at the two of them. "We've been waiting all winter for March. Time to play ball!"

Tad and Conrad sat up. "Are you going to have a team again this year?" Tad asked.

"Of course," David said.

Conrad glanced from David to Daria. "Are you going to let your sister play again?"

David twisted his lips around for a moment, eyeing Daria from the side of his left eye. "I guess so," he finally said.

"She's a good fielder," Conrad said, "even if she is a girl."

"What makes you so sure I want to play on your team?" Daria said.

"Because it's the best team around," David boasted. "We proved that last year."

Tad jumped to his feet. Brushing off his brown cotton trousers, he said, "I heard that TJ is planning to start a team this year."

"Who told you that?" David asked sharply.

"Peter told me. He heard it from Jimmy. Jimmy is thinking about playing for TJ."

"We need Jimmy on second base," David said.

"You'd better talk to him, then," Tad said. "I'm pretty sure he plans to play with TJ."

Conrad still lay in the grass, staring at the sky, but he was listening. "Lars said that he wants to play on your team, but he wants TJ to be the hurler. So if TJ doesn't throw, Lars may not want to play, either."

"What does DJ think?" Tad asked.

Everyone looked at Daria. "Do I have a secret key to DJ's mind?" she said harshly. "You all see DJ just as much as I do."

"But he talks to you," David said.

"Not lately," Daria muttered.

"So what if TJ is going to have a team?" David asked.

127

"We've all known each other since we were little kids. We don't need a couple of outsiders from South Carolina in order to have a good team."

"Without TJ's hurling and DJ's home runs, we won't be the same team we were last year," Conrad said.

"We'll never be able to beat them if they have their own team—with Jimmy at second base."

"Never say never," David said.

"Here they come!" Tad said suddenly.

"Who?"

"TJ and DJ."

The group turned to look in the direction Tad was pointing. Conrad scrambled to his feet. The Baxter twins approached with confident strides.

TJ spoke. "We're starting a baseball team. The first practice is tomorrow. If you want to play, be there after school."

"Does that include everybody?" Conrad asked, glancing doubtfully at David.

TJ shrugged. "If too many people show up, we might have to have tryouts to see who is good enough to play. We want to have a winning team."

"We had a winning team last year," Daria reminded him.

"This new team will be even better."

"Why are you so sure?" David challenged. He smacked a baseball from one hand to the other.

Daria looked anxiously at DJ. Were they going to have to stop another fight?

TJ looked directly at David. "Because I will be in charge."

David stuck his chin out. "Don't act like—"

He did not get to finish his sentence. TJ's mother put an end to the fight before it began. The children's heads all turned toward the street as her ornate black carriage pulled up in front of the school. A hired driver had the reins on the high front seat. Deborah Baxter emerged through the side door and sailed toward the steps of the school building.

"Something's wrong," DJ said quietly.

Daria turned toward him in alarm. "What is it?"

As soon as Mrs. Baxter had identified her sons in the crowd of children, she called their names. "Turner! Donald!"

"She never calls us by our names unless something is wrong," DJ said.

"But we didn't do anything!" TJ protested.

"Turner, Donald, we must go home immediately," Mrs. Baxter said. She gestured urgently that they should come to her.

"What's wrong, Mama?" DJ asked as the group headed toward the steps.

"Come, boys," she commanded.

Daria saw nothing of the soft Southern belle she had seen in Mrs. Baxter before, even when she was arguing with the women's social concerns committee. DJ and TJ were the only children Mrs. Baxter saw on the field that day. She made no gracious comments toward Daria, no flattering remarks about Daria's new spring dress. She did not acknowledge that any of the other boys were there.

"Mama! What's wrong?"

"I must insist that you obey me and come home immediately! I've brought the carriage to take you quickly."

DJ looked at Daria. His gray eyes were lit up with questions.

"Come!" Mrs. Baxter repeated. Her cheeks flamed with anger.

"I'll tell you what's wrong."

Daria and the others spun around to face the voice that promised an answer. Tina stood behind them.

"Daria and David, I think you should come home as well. And the others, all of you should go home."

"Tina?" Daria questioned.

Tina put one around Daria's shoulders and the other around David's.

"South Carolina has seceded from the Union," she said, looking Mrs. Baxter squarely in the eyes.

The children were stunned. During the winter, several Southern states had voted to secede if Mr. Lincoln took office, but the threat had seemed unreal. There had been increasing talk about what would happen if the Southern states actually went through with their threat, but somehow it had felt like something off in the distance. Now it was a reality.

"What's going to happen?" Conrad asked. "Will there be war?"

Tina did not respond. Pulling her siblings in a little closer, she kept her gaze fixed on Mrs. Baxter.

"We must go now," Mrs. Baxter said to her sons, "and I do mean immediately."

TJ and DJ asked no more questions.

Mrs. Baxter marched back to her waiting carriage at a speed Daria had not thought possible in the clothes she was wearing. Her twins had to run to keep up with her.

DJ glanced back over his shoulder at Daria. His gray eyes held no spark and no softness. Instead, Daria looked into deep pools of confusion.

Tina nudged Daria. "Let's go home."

Daria crept along the grayish street. As soon as supper at the Fisk house was over, Daria had slipped out the back door. She had to talk to DJ.

The streets were spooky. Not very many people were out, even though the spring evening was pleasant. She could see the gas lights inside the houses where people had gathered. Daria knew what they were all talking about. Her own family had talked about it over their meal. Could the Southern states really withdraw to form their own country?

Papa had suggested that perhaps Daria and David should stay away from the Baxter boys. There was no point in stirring up more trouble, he said. It would be better to leave the Baxters alone for a while. Perhaps South Carolina would come to its senses in a few weeks.

But Daria would not wait a few weeks. She had to see DJ.

She turned a corner. Now she was finally on the Baxters' street. A few minutes later, she stood at the edge of their property, trying to figure out what to do next. She could not very well march up to the front door, knock loudly, and demand to see DJ. Even the paid household servant who had replaced Mariah would know to send Daria away.

Staying well away from the house, Daria circled around to the back. She had been inside the Baxter house a few times last fall, before TJ and David became such enemies that they could not stand to be in the same room. She was fairly sure she knew which upstairs window was DJ's room.

Daria peered through the darkness, looking for some pebbles. She had not thrown a ball very much over the winter, but if she concentrated and imagined she was in midfield in a baseball game, she could throw a stone and hit the window.

She focused her aim, wound up her arm, and let the pebble fly. The first stone fell short. She got ready with another pebble. This time it hit the mark—the second window from the left on the second floor. Ping! Daria held her breath and waited.

The curtains parted, and a face appeared at the glass. This was too easy, Daria thought.

Then she looked at the face in the window. It was the wrong face! Mrs. Baxter herself was staring into the darkness. Her face was lit up by the lamp in the room. She looked every bit as angry as she had earlier in the afternoon.

Daria let her breath out. Now what was she going to do? She was determined not to leave without talking to DJ, even if it took all night.

She crept closer to the house. She could see shapes moving around behind the curtains, but she had to know whose shapes she was seeing.

Finally, she found a downstairs window with the curtains open. She could see straight through the dining room and into the living room. TJ sat next to the fireplace, talking to his father. Mrs. Baxter joined them with a tray of cookies. Where was DJ?

"Psst."

Daria nearly fell over spinning around.

"What are you doing out here?" DJ demanded. His form was nearly hidden by the bush outside the back door, but he was there.

"How did you know I was out here?" Daria whispered.

His teeth flashed in the darkness. "You don't make a very good sneak. Mama heard a noise while she was upstairs. Then Papa started hearing noises too and thought there was a stray animal out here, so he sent me to check."

Daria let her shoulders sag. "I had to talk to you."

DJ glanced toward the door. "I don't have much time. It doesn't take long to chase away a cat."

Daria got right to the point. "I don't understand all this stuff about South Carolina and the other states not wanting to be part of the country."

DJ shook his head. "You've never been in the South. Northerners don't understand."

"Don't call me a Northerner!" Daria insisted. "I'm your friend, and I'm trying to understand."

"I don't think. . .Mama says. . ." DJ looked at the dirt as he struggled for words. "I don't think Mama is going to let us go back to school. She says she can teach us at home. She never wanted us to go to a Northern school in the first place."

"What is your family going to do?"

"My parents haven't decided yet."

"Will I get to see you anymore?"

"I don't think so."

Daria could not see DJ's eyes in the darkness, but the sadness in his soft voice was plain.

Footsteps clicked across the kitchen floor. Mrs. Baxter appeared in the doorway.

"DJ?"

"Yes, Mama?"

Daria ducked out of sight.

"Did you find a cat?"

"No, Mama. No cat."

"Come back inside then."

"Yes, Mama."

DJ followed his mother back inside with one last look in Daria's direction. Daria had the sinking feeling that this might be the last time she would see DJ Baxter.

Mrs. Baxter shut the door behind her son with a thud. Somehow the night seemed darker.

CHAPTER 15

A Nation at War

More than anything at that moment, Daria wanted to snuggle down deep in her bed and go back to sleep. She pulled the green quilt that served as a bedspread over her head to block out the April light. It was a school day. It would not be long before her mother would trudge up the stairs and insist that she get up. But for now, she squeezed her eyes shut and imagined that it was still dark.

Daria had not slept well. A strange dream had come back three times during the night. It was the same dream that had haunted her several times over the many weeks since she'd last seen DJ.

More than a month had passed since Abraham Lincoln

had been inaugurated as president and moved into the White House. More than a month had passed since South Carolina had officially seceded from the Union. Daria knew her parents hoped that Lincoln could change a lot of things. She just had not expected him to change her friendship with DJ.

The Baxter twins had not returned to school since that March day when South Carolina seceded from the Union. They were not allowed to play with any of the members of the baseball team. In fact, hardly anyone in the Baxter family ever left the house. Mrs. Baxter sent their hired servant out on all the household errands. The Baxter family themselves kept away from the outside Northern world.

And Daria dreamed her strange dream where she stood on an iceberg that was splitting into two pieces. With one foot on each half, she had to choose soon between them or be lost in the icy waters below. She always woke up just before the iceberg cracked wide open.

Every morning, Papa read the newspaper at breakfast. Tina snatched up each section as her father finished it. More and more often, Daria peeked over her sister's shoulder to see the headlines. Every day was the same. The front page was covered with news about the South.

Georgia, Florida, Alabama, Mississippi, Louisiana, and South Carolina had followed through on their promises to separate from the Union if Abraham Lincoln became president. The Southern states were organizing themselves into a new country that the newspaper called the Confederacy. President Lincoln insisted the Confederacy did not exist because the Constitution of the United States did not allow individual states to separate.

Even though the quilt covered Daria's head, daylight seeped into her eyes. She did not want to face another day. If only she could look over Tina's shoulder and read some good news for a change.

The sound of pounding on the front door below her bedroom jolted Daria out of bed. She threw off the quilt and dashed to the window. Shoving it open, she leaned out. Her cousin, Meg Allerton, was beating on the door. What was she doing at the Fisk household so early? Had something happened to Uncle Ben—Meg's papa?

Meg banged on the door steadily until someone opened it. Daria caught a flash of her mother's sleeve as Mama pulled Meg inside.

Daria flew into action. Suddenly she had to know what was going on. Off came her nightgown. She slid into her pantaloons and petticoats and finally pulled her blue cotton school dress over her head and stuffed her feet into her shoes. The pinafore could wait for later, if her mother insisted she wear it. Daria tumbled down the stairs just in time to see her mother hand Meg a mug of coffee in the kitchen.

"The Confederates have fired on Fort Sumter," Meg said.

"What does that mean?" Daria asked, nudging in between Meg and her mother.

Mama motioned that they should all sit down.

"It's an act of war," Charles said quietly. "The Southerners have fired on a United States fort that has protected them in the past."

"But why?" David asked.

"They are no longer part of the Union. So they want the Union military out of their territory."

"According to the newspaper," Papa said, "the Confederates had hoped that the Union troops would leave peacefully."

"How could they do that?" Charles said. "That would be the same as admitting that the Confederacy has a right to exist. President Lincoln would never allow that."

"The fort controls an international port," Papa agreed. "It is important to the independence of the Southern states. But President Lincoln will not let go of it easily."

"Have the troops surrendered?" Charles asked.

Meg shook her head. "Not yet."

Daria did not like the way her stomach felt, all churned up like she had eaten too much chocolate cake.

"The Confederates fired their cannons at 4:30 this morning," Meg said. "April 12, 1861, will be a memorable date."

"Does this mean there is really going to be a war?" Daria asked.

No one spoke. Daria looked around the room, examining every face carefully. She had her answer.

"Do you think the South has a chance to win a war?" Charles asked his father.

Papa shrugged. "It would be seven states against twenty-three. A few more may join the Confederacy before it's all over. The North has a lot of manufacturing to support its effort."

"Where is Fort Sumter?" Daria asked.

"Charleston, South Carolina," Charles answered.

Daria leaped out of her chair and shoved her way past her brothers.

"Where are you going?" her mother asked urgently.

"I have to go out," Daria said. The back door slammed behind her.

She had to see DJ. She would get past any obstacle that Deborah Baxter put in her way.

"Daria, wait!" Tina called.

Daria kept running. As she tore through the streets, Daria sensed the alarm building in Cincinnati. Word was spreading quickly. Many people in Cincinnati were from the South or had relatives in the South. The threat of war was not good news.

At the Baxter house, however, Daria found a different tone. DJ and TJ were out in the front yard in their bare feet, whooping and hollering like they had won a national baseball championship. Daria screamed at them, but they barely heard her. DJ caught her eye for just a second, but then he kept on celebrating.

To see TJ hopping around the yard celebrating a war was not a surprise to Daria. But DJ! How could he be so happy about this?

Ducking to avoid getting hit by arms flying in every direction, Daria forced herself between the Baxter boys. They could no longer ignore her.

"Don't you understand?" she pleaded. "There is going to be a war!"

"The South will get revenge for the way we've been treated," TJ said. "We'll have control of Fort Sumter by tomorrow. Just wait and see. You thought you were so great when Lincoln was elected president. Well, you Northerners can't push us around anymore. We'll show you."

"I never pushed you around at all," Daria insisted. "We were friends, teammates."

"But you are a Northerner."

"Didn't you ever think I was your friend?"

Daria looked from TJ to DJ. TJ ignored the question. As TJ started dancing on the lawn again, DJ said quietly, "Yes, you were my friend."

"I still want to be your friend," Daria said. "We have to talk to your mother and get her to allow us to see each other."

"If you want to see us," TJ called over excitedly, "you'll have to come to South Carolina."

"You're moving?" Daria asked. "But what about the shoe factory?"

"Nothing is certain yet," DJ said.

"Yes, it is," TJ insisted. "I know Mama and Papa. They are Southerners. They are proud of being from South Carolina. And they will not stand by and do nothing when South Carolina needs them."

Daria looked to DJ, who said, "I think he's right. I think we'll go home."

"Is that what you want?" she asked him.

TJ answered for his twin. "Of course it's what he wants. We're proud of being from South Carolina, too. If there is going to be a war, we'll go back and fight it, too."

"But you're only eleven years old! How can you fight a war?"

"We're tall for our age," TJ said. "We could pass for fourteen."

"That is ridiculous!" Daria screamed. "You can't be a soldier. You didn't even do anything to cause this war."

"But I know how to be loyal," TJ said.

Daria looked again at DJ. He nodded. "I know how to

be loyal, too," he said. His gray eyes were steely. Daria had never seen them look that way before.

"This is not a dumb old baseball game," Daria argued. "You're talking about a war. People die in war. Don't you remember anything from the history class at school?"

But the Baxter boys had stopped listening. TJ grabbed a stick from the ground, put it to his shoulder, and pretended to shoot it. He aimed right at Daria.

"Pow!" he said loudly.

Daria jumped. "Stop that!"

"Pow!" he said again.

DJ was scouring the ground for a stick of his own.

Daria stumbled backward, caught her balance, and ran as fast as she could away from the Baxter house. Tears poured from her eyes. She did not even try to stop them. At the end of the block, she saw Tina's familiar red cloak, and she ran straight to her sister's arms.

"They want to kill me!" Daria shrieked.

"Who?"

"TJ and DJ. They have sticks, and they're shooting at me. It's like I was never their friend."

"Daria, I'm so sorry about what happened with the Baxters. They're a nice family, I know they are. War does terrible things to people. It makes them do things they wouldn't do otherwise."

"There wouldn't even be a war if people were not so terrible to each other in the first place." Daria took a deep breath and wiped the tears from her cheek with the back of one hand. She looked back toward the Baxter house. The boys had gone inside. At that moment, Daria Fisk was sure she would never see DJ Baxter again. She did not think she would ever be able to swallow the lump in her throat.

"How can people who believe in God do this?" Daria wanted to know. "Why would they think God wants a war?"

Tina sighed deeply. "Every morning when I read the papers, I ask that question."

"Do you know what God wants you to do in a war?" Daria asked.

Tina shook her head. "No. But I'll find out, and by God's help I'll do it."

They stood silently, watching the Baxter house.

"Let's go home, Daria," Tina said. "Mama was worried when you ran out. You didn't even take a coat."

For the first time, Daria realized she was cold. She shivered against the winter chill of an April morning. Tina took off her cloak and draped it around her sister's shoulders. Daria did not object when Tina gently turned her around and pointed her toward home.

Cincinnati was coming to life for another day. But Daria knew the days would not be ordinary for a long, long time.

There's More!

The American Adventure continues with *Rebel Spy*. As the Civil War begins, David and Daria's lives change. Their father leaves home to serve as a doctor for the Union army, and Mama must open a boarding house to bring in money. Suddenly David and Daria are cleaning rooms, emptying chamber pots, and serving meals as well as going to school.

But Daria is suspicious of one of their boarders. A wounded soldier who claims to know Dr. Fisk, Paul Clark asks lots of questions. Daria is convinced he's a spy, but David thinks he's a great Union hero. When David lets Paul have his horse, is he making a sacrifice for the Union or is he helping a Rebel spy?